DEFIANCE MEANS DEATH

"Let's take them," Slocum whispered to Ames. "Be ready to go in shooting if they don't raise their hands real quick when I order them to."

Ames agreed and moved to the side with his pistol ready. With Ames in position where he wanted him, Slocum straightened to his full six feet and cocked the Colt.

"Throw your hands in the air or die!" he shouted.

"Like hell!" came the defiant reply.

"Damn fool," escaped Slocum's lips as his gun hand jumped into action. The darkness became ablaze with the red-hot muzzle blasts of pistol shots. The cries of someone struck by hot lead filled the night, and the Kid shouted that he surrendered. A heavy fog of black powder smoke hazed the creek bottom as Slocum rushed through the brush, gun in hand, to take the camp . . .

JAKE LOGAN

SLOCUM AND THE SHOSHONE WHISKEY

B

BERKLEY BOOKS, NEW YORK

SLOCUM AND THE SHOSHONE WHISKEY

A Berkley Book / published by arrangement with
the author

PRINTING HISTORY
Berkley edition / March 1995

ISBN: 0-425-14647-2

BERKLEY®
Berkley Books are published by The Berkley Publishing Group,
200 Madison Avenue, New York, New York 10016.
BERKLEY and the "B" design
are trademarks belonging to Berkley Publishing Corporation.

PRINTED IN THE UNITED STATES OF AMERICA

10 9 8 7 6 5 4 3 2 1

1

June, 1876 . . . Smoke from many cooking fires clung close to the ground in the late afternoon air. Squaws tended their kettles and pots over the low flames from driftwood salvaged from the close-by North Platte River or buffalo chips picked up on the prairie. A pack of yellow curs incisively yapped and bit at his horse's heels as Slocum pushed the stout gelding through their camp. Occasionally one of the women looked up with a cold stare at Slocum as he nudged his bay horse.

The lodges and tepees scattered about the village were a strange assortment. Slocum recognized some as Sioux tepees. They belonged to tribesmen whom Chief Sitting Bull called something in his guttural language that translated as *likers-of-white-eyes*. There were Pawnee buffalo-robe lodges stretched over a frame of willows, a Crow tepee or two, lots of tents and canvas structures, and even a few shacks made from packing crates.

Naked children raced about the camp screaming to make themselves heard. They ran pell-mell around tents and tepees in games of tag and you-can't-catch-me. Scolded sharply for their reckless actions by several hard-eyed squaws, they continued unimpeded by the threats. The children's bronze butts shone in the slanting rays of the golden sun about to settle beyond the distant Laramie Peak. They acted disinterested in Slocum's arrival; he liked it that way.

This village was Squaw Town on the west side of Fort Laramie, Wyoming Territory. It was the home of the civilian scouts, some tame Indians who liked to be near the whites and the riffraff that showed up on the frontier— the white men whose names were spelled out on wanted posters in the East, who were anxious to make a quick buck, and not above cutting an innocent person's throat for a two-bit piece. Slocum recalled an old friend's expression about their like: "Why, these lowlifes would sell their own granny to a white slaver for fifty cents and spend half of it for a turn to use her body."

Squaw Town served as the base for the civilian Army scouts and their women, mostly squaws. A large portion of the military guides were white, a few were breeds, and some were full blood Indians. The spawn of the pale-faced scouts were obvious. Redheaded, with bushy hair like an unroached mule, they stuck out from the full bloods. The breeds, young or old, were not readily accepted by either side, white or red. Their fathers wore buckskins, and tracked and translated for the military. They carried their long guns in leather sheaths decorated with fringe and bead work, and except for their white skin, most were hardly more than Indians themselves.

Slocum booted the horse on, hoping to see a familiar face. In the distance, he could view the two-story, white-washed officer barracks and rows of fresh canvas tents that housed the enlisted men. With a purpose in mind, he'd ridden around this village until he knew who was about the fort. The military he didn't fear, but a deputy U.S. marshal or some eager bounty hunter might make his stay around Fort Laramie shorter than Slocum planned.

In the past, Slocum had scouted for the Army. He hoped

to find someone he knew among the rank of the officers, so he could gain employment again. From his count of tents all over the hill and the patrols he'd seen coming there, it seemed that the Army certainly had enough soldiers stationed at the fort. They might need another scout.

A man with shoulder-length white hair came out of a lodge, straightened, and slung a weather-beat felt hat on his head. A look of recognition crossed his face when he saw Slocum. The older man paused to stare narrow-eyed as Slocum approached him.

"Ain't you . . . ?" The man's eyelids were slit like he wasn't certain.

"Slocum," he said, holding the reins high to halt the horse. There was no sense letting the man spell out anything else.

"Pappy Whitcomb," the man behind the scruffy white beard said. He looked pleased to see Slocum. "Why Billy be damn, we did a little," Pap lowered his voice, "hell-raising in the Alabama Second together as I recall."

"Why, you old devil, it's sure good to see you, Sarge," Slocum said, recalling the man. This older man without any front teeth had been a noncom in Slocum's outfit during the war.

"I thought they'd hung you a hundred years ago," Pap said. "Damn, I cried when I heard it the first time. You're a sight for sore eyes."

John acknowledged the man's words with a sharp nod. Carefully he checked around until he felt certain there was no threat close by in the long shadows of the lodges. Anxious to converse privately with his former colleague, Slocum swung out of the saddle, grateful that his boot heels were on the firm ground again. "Thanks, Pap, but they never got me."

"I'm proud. I heard you had big problems after the war."

Pap looked hard at him for confirmation.

"All that's over. Water under the bridge. Is there any law up at the sutler's post or any bounty hunters around here?" Slocum tossed his head toward the hill and the fort. "A man can't be too careful under the best of circumstances."

"I know what you mean." Pap scrubbed his mouth with his palm as if considering the question, then shook his head to dispel any concern. "Nothing we can't handle." He let fly a cud of brown tobacco to the side. "Slocum, huh? That's what you call yourself these days?"

"Yes, Slocum. Solves lots of problems for me."

"No doubt. Your secret's safe with me. What in the hell are you doing here?"

"Want to try my hand at poker for starters. My pockets are a little dry. Then I need to find a money-making deal. I've done some scouting before. I've even got some recommends in my saddlebags that might get me hired on again. What's your game here?"

"Anything ain't too dishonest that will make me a buck. I've freighted a lot, drove some cattle, scouted some for the Army, but them blue bellies get hard to stomach day in day out, don't they?" Pap squinted his eyes as if being around the blue uniforms for extended periods was more than he could stand.

"I agree. You say it's all clear up there? Let's go up to the sutler's. I'll buy the whiskey."

"Slocum, that sounds like a helluva deal."

"Where can I put my horse?" Slocum looked around.

"There's a boy here will take care of him. Just stow your gear in my place," Pap said, motioning to the lodge. "Woman! Get out here."

Slocum saw her round brown eyes as she parted the flap. The short, thick-waisted Indian girl could not have been older than sixteen by Slocum's calculations. Dressed in fancy fringed buckskin with lots of trade beads for decoration, she hurried past Pap and held out her arms for Slocum's saddle and gear.

"She's Delaware-Fox," Pap said with his thin chest stuck out. "Her name's Morning Woman. Cost me ten horses, but by damn she's a good worker. Tell you something else, she's hotter in bed than a four-burner cast-iron stove plumb full of split chinquapin wood." Pap cackled and gave her a friendly swat on the butt when she went by him laden with Slocum's saddle, pads, and bedroll. She winked back mischievously at Whitcomb, before ducking to enter the lodge.

"Billy Boy!" Pap shouted to a breed. The youngster who answered him came running. He wore a loincloth so Slocum guessed him to be well into his teens.

"Take care of this horse." Pap took the lariat from Slocum and gave the lead to the boy. "My friend will pay you well, but only if the horse's belly is full of rich grass and well watered when he returns. Otherwise he will shoot off one of your toes." Pap pointed to the boy's foot.

"I take care for him," the boy said proudly.

"You just remember," Pap said, then made a clicking sound with his tongue, "no toe, if you don't do it right or if that horse gets stolen.

"Come on," he added, sounding impatient to be going on. "Don't worry one minute, Billy Boy won't let anything happen to that horse of yours."

Slocum hardly heard the man's reassurance about the boy's capability or his horse's care. He was too busy watching an Indian woman ride past on a bald-face horse. She was tall by Indian standards, wearing a yellow doe-skin blouse that outlined her well-developed form. A good deal of shapely leg showed below the fringed hem of her skirt and above her calf-high moccasins. She rode a high cantle saddle covered in snowy elk hide. This was no everyday squaw. Her raven-black hair hung down her back in long braids decorated with small blue feathers.

"Who the hell is that?" Slocum asked.

"Shoshone, nobody knows much about her." Pap spit to the side and then wiped his mouth on his sleeve. "She's damn sure a looker, ain't she?" The old man chuckled to himself as if impressed by her beauty.

Slocum agreed as he turned back for one more longing look after her. He wanted to know more about the Shoshone squaw. His empty gut rolled over as he considered her ripe body under the deerskin.

"What the hell is a Shoshone doing here?" he finally asked. "Why, the closest reservation is clear up on the Wind River."

"Damned if I know. But she sure would make a bed full," Pap said as they hiked on through the camp.

Slocum turned for a last glimpse of her, but she was gone from view. He resumed his walking, still wondering about the woman and her business there. She certainly had lots of damn interesting mystique about her. He swore she'd nearly smiled at him when he first saw her, like she knew him. He wished he'd paid her more attention at the start. What the hell, she was probably some old chief's wife anyway. The notion of tasting good whiskey and even eating some food might be more settling than taking on some hot-blooded fine-looking squaw anyway. Slocum drew a deep breath to help let the notion of the woman pass as he and the old man quickly strode up the long grassy grade toward the white two-story barracks next to the commissary structure. He mused over how either Pap needed a drink awfully bad or the man was anxious for some other reason to get there.

Fort Laramie's sutler's post was a low-roofed building sprawling across the hillside. The walls were built partially of adobe bricks made on the site, plus rocks and cottonwood logs in a random form that always made Slocum wonder if the builders were drunk when they put it up. The original fort had been made of adobe with high walls and gates, but the adobe had seriously eroded in wet years and melted away. The Army purchased the trading post after the war and shortly began to build two-story officer quarters and eventually other barracks. A company of engineers and an on-site sawmill made the lumber from logs brought from Laramie Peak sixty miles away. Each time he passed through Laramie, Slocum noticed the changes brought to this military outpost. Since his first visit there over a decade before, they'd made many improvements.

The original purpose of the outpost was to protect the wagon trains headed west. Slocum, like the Indians, had decided those caravans would never stop coming. Oregon-bound dirt farmers and merchants brought their white canvas-topped wagons powered by sluggish oxen. Slocum had ridden by them all day to get there. They were camped by the thousands all down the valley of the North Platte. The parked wagons went for miles while they rested their oxen for the hard push ahead, traded for fresh teams, and bought supplies from the various businesses set up down the river bottom to administer to them.

Slocum ducked his head to enter the store after Pap. When he straightened inside the door casing, he felt grateful to finally be there. He had no reason to mix with those migrants in the valley; the folks inside the barroom-store were his kind. The cigar smoke was as thick as fog on a fall morning. The sweet perfume of whiskey mixed with the sour wine smell of horse and the unbathed, camp fire–stinking men, all under the fluttering coal-oil lamps hung on the low log rafters.

"What'll it be, gents?" the bartender asked, with the sleeves of his white shirt constricted by red garters.

"A bottle of good whiskey and two glasses," Slocum said and dug in his pocket for the money. He had only a fast glimpse of the room filled with tables of men playing cards and seriously drinking.

There were minutes like this, when a man first arrived in such a place and he didn't know for certain that his worst enemy wouldn't pop up—scraping the chair legs on the floor, maybe even spilling the chair over with a clatter in his haste, and then demanding satisfaction with his hand riding his gun butt. Slocum's muscles tensed awaiting such a move by some faceless individual in the room full of those men busy discarding pasteboards or betting with the clink of coins tossed atop others.

"There's a vacant table by the wall," Pap said and led the way.

"Fine." Slocum followed him. Nothing looked out of place, nor did any of the sideways glances at him appear hostile. Old habits were hard to shake, but caution had been his hole card, so for the meanwhile he would watch closely to be certain there was no threat in the room. Slocum eased his tall frame into the chair with his back to the wall, not touching the whiskey, waiting to see if anyone would challenge him.

"You've done some hard riding," Pap said, reaching for the bottle.

"Staying alive hasn't been easy," Slocum said and relaxed a little.

Pap splashed liquor in their tumblers and raised his glass for a toast. "Here's to better days."

"I'll drink to that."

"Why, you cheating tinhorn!" A young soldier jumped to his feet at a nearby table. "You got to be cheating winning all that money off me."

"Son, you better be backing some of that hard talk with

a gun," the accused man in the ruffled shirt and frock coat said, rising easy.

Slocum studied the man. A little balding in the front, with his hat cocked back, he had the pallor of a man who lived inside, out of the sun and wind. The gambler was past thirty, so he obviously knew his way around. Most gaming men never lived that long. Either an irate soldier losing his month's pay or some other sore loser usually got lucky and killed them before their thirtieth birthday. This man knew how to survive; he'd probably even cheated the ignorant youth.

"What are you going to do?" Pap whispered, looking taken back by Slocum's interest in the confrontation. "Do you aim to horn in on their argument?"

"No. Nothing in it for me, it ain't my war. I just want to play cards with that man."

"Hell," Pap said under his breath, "you heard that soldier say he cheated."

"I know. Still I think my luck is strong tonight." Slocum watched as some of the private's flunkies escorted him outside. They'd talk some sense into the young man's head.

With a scowl on his face, the gambler settled back down in his seat, reshuffling his deck of cards.

"What the hell has luck got to do with cheating?" Pap asked Slocum with a frown poised over his raised glass.

"Everything if you use it right." Slocum stood up with the drink in his hand. He wanted a chance at this fleecer of young, inexperienced soldiers. The man, of course, could be innocent of all charges; Slocum intended to find out and try his own luck at the same time.

"I'll bring the whiskey bottle, go ahead," Pap said and shook his head like he didn't believe they were going to do it.

"You dealing those cards or just shuffling them?" Slocum

asked the gambler as he stood before him with the glass in hand.

The gambler looked up at Slocum mildly. Swiftly he shifted the deck from hand to hand in a false shuffle that Slocum didn't miss.

"My name's Ames, have a seat." The gambler offered Slocum the chair with a gesture of his hand holding the cards. "You're new around here."

Slocum just nodded. He had started to pull the chair out when a loud individual burst in the doorway. Forced to turn and view the owner of the foul mouth, Slocum observed a brawny man wearing a patch over one eye and a hard look in his good eye, standing with his feet apart inside the doorjamb. His gold earring reminded Slocum of a seagoer. The wide red belt of felt material girdling the man's waist was festooned with pistol and knife handles. The stranger s buckskins were grimy with smoke, grease, and dirt. He had a thin, scraggly beard on his jaw, and he scowled contemptuously at the room full of men. Silence ruled the barroom as everyone patiently but intently waited for the intruder's next move.

"Well, you scruffy dogs, is there a man among you wants to fight me?" the stranger demanded. "I've killed the likes of all of you in here with me bare fists."

"Elijah Hawkins! Raise your hands slow like!" a booming voice commanded from behind the bar. Slocum recognized the twin barrels of a ten-gauge scattergun as the gun bearer continued his directions. "Put those irons of yours on the bar and prepare to act like a civilized man in my post or meet your maker! What'll it be?"

"Why, dear Ezra my man." The stranger's face softened as he spoke to the sutler. "I was only funning these guys." He did obey the sutler and moved to the bar, where he began to remove his weapons.

"I don't consider you coming in here bragging and challenging my customers to a fight like that as funning. Mind your manners in my store, Hawkins, or I'll blast you to hell. Am I clear?"

"Clear as the morning on the prairie, sir. May I have my guns back?"

"When you leave you can," the tall sutler said, putting the scattergun down on its butt as he surveyed Hawkins's arsenal of various firearms and knives piled on top of the bar.

Slocum sat down, satisfied that the matter of the bullying stranger was settled. From the corner of his eye, he noticed three others slip inside who appeared to be with Hawkins. They bought bottles at the bar and slunk off to a corner table with the man. The shifty-eyed threesome reminded Slocum of weasels, scared of their own shadows but vicious as anything when cornered or on the attack. He turned his attention back to the game.

"Ames is my name."

"Slocum's mine."

"Five card fine?"

"Deal me in," Pap said to Ames, setting the whiskey bottle down and taking a seat. Hawkins's actions in the rear of the room obviously kept some of the old man's attention, for Pap studied that portion of the store closely before he turned back to the game.

"Staying here long?" Ames asked Slocum as he set down the deal in front of Pap for a cut. That courtesy completed, Ames began to deal the cards on the table.

"Long enough. This is Pap. We did some farming together years ago," Slocum said, studying his hand and wondering if it was worth two bits.

"I was raised on a farm. Hated that damn drudgery. Didn't you?" Ames asked.

"Two bits," Slocum said, wondering if his pair of sixes could even start a winning hand. "I never minded farming. It was the distractions like the foreclosing bankers and tax people that bothered me."

"Yeah," Pap said, tossing in his bet. "It was the distractions that made farming bad."

"We had them bastards, too. You two ain't looking for work, are you?" Ames asked.

"Doing what?" Slocum asked, discarding three cards.

"I have a herd of brood mares to deliver up on the Wind River, to a rancher. I could use someone that's handy with a gun." The gambler looked directly at Slocum.

"What makes you think I'm your man?"

"I saw you come in. I know men like you. That gun you're wearing isn't a Christmas tree ornament."

"I'll take two cards," Pap said, a little impatient with Ames, who seemed to be waiting on an answer from Slocum.

Slocum fanned out his new cards in his hand; the third six was there. "I'll bet another quarter."

"How much you two charge me to deliver them?" Ames asked before he lifted his three cards.

"Half the deal's gain," Slocum said. "What does it pay?"

"If I can get those mares to my buyer up there, they'll bring forty dollars a head."

"That 'if' bull crap is mighty tough to stir. The Wind River I know is a powerful long ways from here," Pap said, with a disapproving head shake as he tossed in his money. "Why, there's enough scalping Injuns and desperadoes in the country between here and there to whup an army."

Ames drew in a sharp breath and looked ruefully at his hand. "That's why I have been staying here the last two weeks. Looking for a couple good men. You look like an adventuresome man, Slocum. I'll let you deliver those horses and we'll split the profit."

"Three sixes," Slocum said, hardly hearing the man's offer.

"Beats me," Pap said and tossed in his hand. Ames nodded in defeat and discarded his hand.

"How do we know you got a deal to sell those horses for that much?" Slocum asked, leaning back and tasting the harsh whiskey in his tumbler. This man Ames might have just what he needed for a new grub stake. Pap seemed to know something about the country up there. Slocum's knowledge of the Wind River was slim; he'd only passed through the country going west. He'd never been in the upper end where the Mountain Men used to hoot and have their rendezvous every year.

"Good, you're interested," Ames said, shuffling the cards.

"Always, but not in horse wrangler wages," Slocum said to set the man on the right course.

"Another thing, mister, that's a good place to get an arrow in your ass or your manhood separated from your corpse," Pap said before spitting on the floor.

Ames looked a little pale at the old man's words. He dealt the next hand, and Slocum watched the dealer pick up his cards before he did the same. So far he had not detected anything out of the ordinary about Ames's dealing.

"I'll pass," Slocum said, looking up. The ace-jack looked like loners in a sea of small cards.

"Two bits," Pap said and looked eager to wager.

Pap won another small pot. At this rate, they'd be a week winning enough to barely exist on, Slocum figured as he studied the next five cards.

"Where them mares at?" Slocum asked.

"Twenty miles east. No feed left to graze them on around here. I got some sodbuster watching them."

"I may get a chance to go look them over. How do I find them?" Slocum asked.

"Just ride east till you get where there's a deep cut in the bluff on the north side, and you'll see a side road. 'Gustafson' is on one of the boards posted there. He's holding the mares for me."

"Who's buying them in the Wind River country?"

"You taking my deal to deliver them?" Ames asked.

"Just learning enough to make a sensible decision."

"We playing poker or you going to jaw all night about them damn horses?" Pap asked.

"I fold," Slocum said and dumped his hand on the table.

"Me, too," Ames said.

"Sonsabitches and me with a full house, aces and tens."

"Better have another drink of that rotgut whiskey," Slocum said and clapped the man on the shoulder. "It'll settle you some."

Pap poured himself a half glass then set the bottle down and corked it. He looked skeptically at the new deal before him and then took a larger drink. In deep thought, Pap wiped his mouth on his sleeve before he swept up his cards in one hand.

"That man Hawkins offered to take them up there," Ames said under his breath. "However, I figured I'd never see my horses or the money again."

"That's for sure," Pap grumbled and waited for Slocum to pitch in his quarter. "That's the biggest bunch of no-accounts in the country back there. Quarter Martin is the big one; he's got a wife stays on their homestead. Say he killed four men in Tennessee. The kid in the bunch is Robbie Muldone. He's a drunk robber, sneak thief. I caught him messing around with some little Injun girl down by the river and told him I'd cut him if I ever caught him bothering her again."

"That breed, Black Dog" Ames said, being careful to lower his voice, "is the one killed two men at Sugar Crossing."

"Nice guys. They could probably deliver those mares for you. They sound tough enough," Slocum said, pitching in a quarter.

"Yeah, I'd never live to spend the money either," Ames said, covering the bet after Pap tossed his in. Ready to deal new cards, the gambler sat with the deck in his hand.

"You do have a problem, Ames," Slocum said. "Three cards, I want a better hand this time."

"Me, too," Pap said.

"Would you buy them from me and deliver them yourself?" Ames asked.

"How much?" Slocum said, looking at his new cards but with his ears alert for the man's price.

"Thirty bucks a head?"

"Fifteen?"

"That's all that Hawkins offered." Ames slumped in the chair with a rueful shake of his head and studied his hand. "I brought them mares in from Texas. Plus I paid two drovers good wages to bring them up here. Then they got some wild notion about a gold strike in the Black Hills and left me."

"Tell you what," Slocum said, "Pap and I'll go look at them in the morning. Then I'll tell you what I'm going to do and will pay."

"Fair enough, I'll take you out there. Need to check on them anyway."

"Hey, Ames," someone interrupted them. "You ready to sell those mares?"

Peeved at the man's abrupt intrusion, Slocum looked up at the bulk of Hawkins's body. He wore the smell of camp smoke and an almost putrid odor of rancid bear grease. As Hawkins drummed the tabletop, Slocum saw that his hands were dirt-stained and his fingernails were rimmed in black.

"No, I ain't selling to you at that price," Ames said, acting busy with his cards.

"My price is better than the magpies eating them."

"You a horse buyer?" Slocum asked, setting his cards facedown on the table. First, he had no notion of the man seeing them, and second, he wanted to have the use of both hands if Hawkins started something.

"Sure I buy horses. I buy women, gold, whiskey. Who the hell are you?"

Slocum shook his head to dismiss the man's concern. "Just passing through, nobody you know."

"You got a name? Smith, huh, that's your name?" Hawkins laughed out loud. "Hey, we got a new Mr. Smith here tonight!" His laughter grew louder and more raucous.

Pap gave Slocum a quick head shake to discourage him from striking out. Slocum knew the ex noncom knew exactly what was going on inside his head—his plan to silence the man: drive a piston-size fist in Hawkins's belly and then crack his skull with the whiskey bottle off their table while he was bent over hugging his guts.

"You don't think none of that is funny?" Hawkins asked, sobering.

"Not one part of it," Slocum said, soft enough to force the big man to strain to hear it.

"Well, what are you going to do about it?"

"Let Ezra throw you out," Slocum said.

"Huh!" Hawkins whirled around in time to see the raw-boned sutler with the small carved bat in his hand coming at a deliberate pace down the front of the bar.

"I'm leaving! I'm leaving!" Hawkins protested and took several steps backward to the door. "Dammit, that man insulted me! That Smith guy!"

"I told you if you insulted my customers or caused trouble in here again, you were out! Now, get out and take that scum of yours out, too!" Ezra pointed to the door with the club, still short of batting distance. Hawkins seemed to appreciate the weapon and moved fast enough to save any licks by the sutler.

Slocum turned his attention back to the poker game; the situation was in hand. One thing he knew for certain, he hadn't seen the last of Hawkins or the hard-eyed bunch that gave him cold stares when they passed him to catch up with their boss.

"Aces, a pair," Pap bragged as he fanned out his cards to show them. His look went sour, however, when John laid out three queens and took the pot. "They ain't had their last word." Pap tossed his head toward the doorway to indicate Hawkins's bunch.

Slocum agreed after a quick sideways glance at their backs. A biting dog either had to be taught better or shot.

2

The cool morning breeze washed Slocum's face as the three men rode abreast past the long lines of covered wagons. Ames wore his small derby and brown suit, and Pap was in his buckskins. Slocum was dressed in his drover clothing: a wide-brimmed felt hat, vest, canvas waist overalls, and a collarless blue shirt. All three men wore their pants inside their boot tops.

Some of the trains had begun to move out, folks headed west. The wooden wagon boxes creaked noisily as they tilted and strained, rocking from side to side on the even road. A metallic roll vibrated through the air as the iron rims on the ruts were drawn inches forward by oxen. A quick passage of a cold front the night before had sprinkled the area with light showers, but the drops quickly evaporated as the fiery sun cracked the horizon. Slocum, Pap, and the gambler were headed east to look over Ames's Texas mares.

"Enough damn pilgrims leaving today, ain't they?" Pap said as they rode against the trains' westward flow.

"They must be a million folks want to live in Oregon," Ames said, shaking his head in disgust.

"Nice country but the good land's already claimed out there," Slocum said, standing in the stirrups to stretch his legs. "These folks will only find dry sagebrush and bunchgrass to homestead on when they get there."

"No gold either. Take them folks going north out there." Ames swung around to point out the long line of wagons heading northeast. "They're going to get rich in the Black Hills. Custer said there's millions of dollars in gold nuggets up there."

"Why ain't you headed there then?" Slocum asked.

"I've got these mares to deal with or I would. You two act like you don't believe Colonel Custer's gold story." Ames looked at the two of them in amazement.

"Damn sure don't. I think that red-faced sumbitch is a liar and a braggart besides," Pap said.

"You know him?" Ames asked, looking dismayed.

"I saw him in action in Kansas three years ago. He shot up Injun camps and called it war. Besides that he's a squaw killer." Pap quieted down after that and looked straight ahead like the matter was settled for his part.

"I don't figure there is anything wrong with making love to a squaw," Slocum said to egg the older man on. "Last time I checked, that gal in your tepee was red skinned."

"I never killed them like Custer did. I paid ten good damn horses for her, too." Pap's neck became red as he flexed it in his collar.

"Why, I ain't opposed to a squaw in my bedroll. Are you, Ames?" Slocum asked.

Ames just laughed and they rode on. Pap never said another word. The three touched their hat brims in passing for the number of women that they met in sunbonnets, tramping on the road beside their wagons. Fat gals, ugly ones, hard lookers, and soft ones, some were heavy pregnant and others skinny as a rail. Oregon-bound wives, Slocum noted, going to populate a new land with their menfolks. There were enough males at that. They were whipping the air to make their steers pull, and cussing them.

Slocum dreamed of a place of his own someday—a wife, children, and a good farm—but as he drew a deep breath, he knew the truth. Such a life would never happen to Slocum. He was cursed to ride on, looking over his shoulder for another bounty hunter on his tail or law that wanted his hide tacked to the barn door.

They reached the homestead by mid-morning. The sun had grown hotter. Coming from the south again, the eternal wind swept their horses' tails around to their stirrups when they reined up before the soddy in the hillside. A small cloud of dust puffed up from their horses' feet.

"Hello, Mrs. Gustafson," Ames said, leaning forward in the saddle to greet the woman in the doorway.

Tall and hardly more than a girl, Mrs. Gustafson emerged into the sun wearing a gray dress. The wind-blasted material clung to the large ball in the center of her belly where the next heir rested in her womb. Her thin, long face showed much concern as she held her long, dark hair back from her face to speak.

"Thank God you're here, Mr. Ames. They stole the horses last night. My husband went after them alone." Her brown eyes were close to tears.

"How long ago?" Slocum asked, considering her concern for the man as well founded. A dirt farmer was no match for the outlaw element that would have stolen Ames's mares.

"My man only has a twenty-two," she said as she risked raising one of the arms that had held down her wind-pressed dress, to point northward. "He left to trail them early this morning."

"Go inside, ma'am, and don't you worry," Slocum said softly to comfort her. "We'll find your man and bring him back safely." She turned to obey him, and the men charged their horses at the hill.

"Wonder who took my horses," Ames said as they spurred their mounts up the hillside.

"Damned if I know," Pap said. He glanced apprehensively in the direction of the woman they'd left standing at the doorway. "We'll be lucky as hell if she don't have that young'un while we're out looking for her man."

Slocum silently agreed.

They whipped their horses and topped the ridge above the soddy dug in the hill. Only a crooked metal stovepipe stuck up as a hint anyone lived like a prairie dog under the sod.

Ahead of them lay an unending rolling brown sea of grass that swept as far as they could see. No sign of the horses or Gustafson. Wind hard on his back, Slocum studied the distance for a telltale sign of dust. Nothing.

"Spread out. They left tracks," Slocum said. "There will be signs for us to follow."

"Damn," Ames swore. "I never figured they'd get stolen this close to all those wagon camps and the business."

"Listen here," Pap said, jerking his horse up short to walk. "There's damn hostiles come every night and steal things out from under folks' noses around here. Hell, they probably ain't camped more than ten miles from here."

"You figure Injuns got them?" Ames asked.

"Not unless they ride shod horses," Slocum said, straightening up in the saddle from reading some sign on the ground. "Couple of shod horses herded them."

"White men, huh?" Ames asked.

"Mangy white men," Pap said before he spit sideways. "I got less use for a horse thief than I do a flea-bit dog."

"They've got some use for them mares," Slocum said, carefully scanning the horizon. "They may even be taking them to the Wind River if they know the place to collect the money for them."

"Guess they could ask when they got there and find out in a damn quick minute," Pap said, spitting again. "Ain't many folks up there would be in the market for high-priced mares."

"You're saying I've talked too much, huh?" Ames said, looking crestfallen at the notion he'd lost his investment.

"You could have talked less," Pap said with a nod. "Place like Fort Laramie it don't hurt to keep the damn cards to your chest."

"Trouble is I know about gambling. I don't know a damn thing about horse trading. I just saw a chance to make some big bucks, and, well, like all wild deals there was more risk in it than I figured on." Downcast, Ames stared in defeat at his saddle horn.

"No time to cry over spilt milk," Slocum said. "We better ride or that dirt farmer is going to be lying dead out there. He damn sure ain't not match for rustlers."

They headed northwest, and the hooves of their horses pounded the grassland as they loped along. With the prairie wind sweeping his face, Slocum considered all the things he knew about the horse deal. Several no-accounts had learned about Ames's business. However, one thing stuck out in Slocum's mind as they rode hard on the rustler's backtrail: Hawkins and his threat from the night before that the magpies would eat the mares if he didn't get to take them up to the Wind River and collect the profit. Somehow the belligerent man and his henchmen were involved in the theft. No Indian party took the horses. The tracks trailing the herd were shod animals. Iron shoes meant white men, and Slocum felt certain that if Hawkins wasn't in on the rustling, he'd planned it. He urged the big bay horse on. They didn't have supplies to chase these thieves to the far side of Wyoming, so they needed to capture them quickly.

In late afternoon, Slocum spotted a lone rider ahead.

He could tell by the choppy gait that the man rode a workhorse.

"That's Gustafson!" Ames said.

"Good," Slocum said, feeling relieved that they had overtaken the dirt farmer.

The man was hatless. His shock of brown wind-tossed hair gave him an even wilder look as he cautiously studied their approach. His eye were slits above his full beard. He balanced the .22 rifle on his knee as he reined in his big draft horse. The gray animal snorted gratefully, his shoulders lathered with sweat. Drips ran off the gray horse's belly and chest as Slocum and the others drew rein before the man.

"Who has my mares?" Ames asked.

Gustafson shook his head. "Don't know. They are still ahead. They took them before dawn. Woke me up when I heard the sound of the bell mare, and I tried to stop them. It was dark, and when I ran up there they shot at me. I didn't have my gun."

"Take something bigger than that twenty-two to stop rustlers," Pap said.

"All I have." The farmer gave Pap a cold look. "I have killed three Injuns with it since I come here."

"Hell, guess I ain't that smart about guns." Pap shrugged.

"How many rustlers are there?" Slocum asked the man as he pushed his horse in closer.

"Three, maybe four. I never saw much in the dark."

"Were they wearing hats?" Slocum asked.

"Yes, sir, why you asking?"

"Because we figured they're white men and not Indians."

"That's what I thought when I seen them," the farmer agreed. "Injuns always scream and hoop a lot when they steal something. Kinda like they want to brag about it. These guys cussed and shot at me when I shouted for them to stop."

"You better go home and see about that woman of yours. We can handle this," Slocum said.

"She having pains?" Gustafson asked. His blue eyes opened wide.

"She looks like she's close," Slocum said.

"Here, let me pay you for keeping them," Ames said and reached in his vest pocket for some money.

"I can't take your money since they stole them horses in my care."

"Do it for that newborn coming," Ames said, holding out his hand with the coins.

The sodbuster looked undecided but finally shrugged and took the money.

"I sure appreciate you, Mr. Ames, and you fellows, too. I can shoot the eye out of a rabbit with this gun if you need me."

"Go see about her, she needs you. We can handle this," Slocum said to reassure the man as he shook his hand and they exchanged names. Ira Gustafson was the man's full name. Perhaps there would be another Ira by the time he returned to his soddy and wife.

"I never run from a fight," the man said proudly.

"We know," Pap said to reassure him they did not mean to doubt his bravery. "We'll be seeing you."

Ames thanked the man again and they loped off, leaving the farmer to turn his large-footed horse southward and head back. John returned the farmer's wave from the rise. He felt better about the man returning home to help his wife have their child. Rustlers were his and Pap's game. The threesome galloped their mounts northward.

The sun's last red rays were long when they dropped their hard-breathing horses to a walk. Pap had spoken of a creek somewhere ahead where the rustlers would probably water and rest their stock for the night.

"Dead Cow Branch, they call it," Pap said as they walked their sweaty, winded mounts. "Lots of cottonwoods and willows. I've been there a few times. Can't be more than a few miles."

"We'll have some cover at night," Slocum said, recalling that the quarter moon had been slow to rise in the past few evenings.

"What if there's a lot of them?" Ames asked.

Pap spit to the side like he didn't hardly consider the question worthy a reply. "Don't make much difference, we're taking them mares back. That's what we come for, ain't it?"

"Sure but—"

"Pap means," Slocum interrupted, "we ain't taking any less than those mares back and it really doesn't matter if the whole gang is there."

Ames nodded quickly, but Slocum could see the man had reservations about the impending confrontation. He'd already admitted he was a gambler and not in his element out there in the horse business. Still Slocum felt certain the man was steady enough to stand with him and Pap in a fight. No one ever went into battle entirely convinced they'd live to see the next dawn. From time to time Slocum felt the same twangs of doubt pull on him before riding into a challenge where men could die. Never mattered how piss poor his future looked for having the life he always dreamed of, Slocum still enjoyed his fast living too much to take many unnecessary chances.

"Have some jerky," Slocum said, holding out the brown twists of peppered dried beef he'd taken from his saddle-bag.

"I better not break my teeth on this," Pap said, taking a strip. "I ain't got many left to lose."

"You won't. A white woman made it from a young buffalo cow I shot for her," Slocum said.

"Thanks," Ames said as he selected a piece.

"I figure," Slocum said. Then he paused to gnaw off a hunk, starting to soften it with his saliva as he slowly bit the meat. "We need to hold up short of that creek. Wait till dark, and after we scout the lay of their setup, then we can rush them."

Pap agreed as he chewed away on the jerky.

"Sure," Ames said. "I just never did no soldiering."

"You weren't in the war?" Pap asked with a sharp frown.

"Oh yes, but I guarded the hometown courthouse down there in Texas. We was home guard in case of insurrection or if any behind-the-lines parties tried to attack."

"Gawdamn, I bet they had deeds and everything in that courthouse to protect," Pap said.

"That was where he was assigned," Slocum said with a frown at the older man. "You went where you were assigned."

"I gawdamn sure didn't have no pisspot courthouse to guard either during the damn war," Pap said.

"Hell, at least he ain't no blue belly." Slocum shared a private head shake for Ames not to be worry about Pap and his ranting.

The bell mare's clang carried softly across the night. Ames gave Slocum a nod of recognition as they crept closer to the camp and the fire. His Colt in his hand, Slocum stole his way ahead in a half crouch, leading the gambler. The men before them in camp were talking openly. They must have felt certain there was no pursuit. Slocum raised his gun barrel as a sign to halt and then turned his ear to listen.

" . . . where in the Wind River we got to go?"

"He said he'd find out . . ." The rattle of pans covered the man's last words.

"Why ain't he here and paying us?"

"Shut up, Kid, he'll be here before midnight."

"What if we get caught doing this?" the young voice whined.

"You'll hang! Hell, if you get caught by citizens, that's what they do to horse thieves. Listen, we ain't getting caught, Kid. There ain't any law within a hundred miles of here, and they ain't got no time to screw around with horse thieves."

Who was coming at midnight? Slocum wondered if they could capture the leader, too. Probably Hawkins himself was riding out to pay them and take possession of the herd. Were there three or four men in camp? Slocum wasn't certain. One was nighthawking the horses; he was Pap's responsibility. There still might be someone else besides the two he could hear talking.

"We get our money and we head straight for the Black Hills," a gruff voice said, and Slocum saw the last man's broader form as the other two stood around and inspected the pot by the firelight's glow. Good, there were only three in camp. Slocum held up that many fingers, and Ames silently agreed.

Should they wait until the man who hired them showed or should they do something? Slocum drew a deep breath. If Hawkins brought his gang in addition to these three outlaws, the three of them might have a gun battle they couldn't win.

"Let's take them," Slocum whispered to Ames. "Be ready to go in shooting if they don't raise their hands real quick when I order them to."

Ames agreed and moved to the side with his pistol ready. With Ames in position where he wanted him, Slocum straightened to his full six feet and cocked the Colt.

"Throw your hands in the air or die!" he shouted.

"Like hell—" came the defiant reply.

"Damn fool" escaped Slocum's lips as his gun hand jumped into action. The darkness became ablaze with the red-hot muzzle blasts of pistol shots. The cries of someone struck by hot lead filled the night, and the Kid shouted that he surrendered. A heavy fog of black powder smoke hazed the creek bottom as Slocum rushed through the brush, gun in hand, to take the camp.

"You all right?" Ames asked as he joined him.

"Fine," Slocum said as he faced the wide-eyed Kid with his hands high. Another rustler was silently slumped over a saddle on the ground. From the position of his body, Slocum was satisfied that the outlaw across the saddle was dead. The third one moaned and held his shoulder. Slocum kicked aside his handgun on the ground.

"What you going to do with us?" the terrified Kid—in his late teens—asked.

More shots out on the prairie forced Slocum to turn his ear toward the drum of spooked horses.

"That's Pap," he said confidently to the gambler.

"He need our help?" Ames asked, busy disarming the Kid.

"Pap Whitcomb don't need help getting one rustler," Slocum said with a smile in the corner of his mouth.

"What you going to do to us?" the Kid screamed.

"Shut up," the wounded outlaw said from his seat on the ground. "They're going to hang us, I told you so."

"Oh, no!" the youth cried.

Pap rode in and dropped off his horse. "We won't need no rope for that one out there. He's gone to his reward."

"Good enough," Slocum said. "We'll tie these two up and wait for the buyer they talked about coming. By the way, Kid, who's coming to pay you for the horses?"

"You shut up, Kid! Don't tell him nothing. You die like a damn man, not some chicken-livered sumbitch," the wounded rustler swore before he broke into a hard cough. Pap stepped in and swiftly kicked the man hard in the chest with his boot toe, for his effort to silence the youth.

"I don't want to die, mister!"

"Who's coming to pay you for these damn horses you stole?" Slocum demanded.

"Elijah Hawkins," the Kid said and dropped to his knees, holding his bound hands up in a prayerlike action. "Please dear God I'll do anything. Don't hang me for God's sake. My momma thinks—"

"Kid," Pap said, "we let you go, why, you'd be stealing someone else's damn horse in less than a week. Like a gawdamn chicken-killing dog, ain't a thing a man can do about it but end it."

A silence fell on the camp as Ames and Slocum gagged the two bound prisoners.

"What now?" Ames asked.

"We take turns nighthawking those horses. They scatter very much, Pap?" Slocum asked.

"No, sir."

"You two were in the Army together," Ames said, making a discovery. "I heard it just then when Pap said, 'No, sir.' "

"We were a long time ago," Slocum said with a grim nod. "Tonight we need to be sure that Hawkins don't slip up on us. He might not have intended to pay these guys either. Be like what I've seen of him so far to just double-cross and kill these four. Then he'd not have to compensate a soul to own your mares."

"Good notion," Pap said, "we're damn sure dealing with a real backstabber. I'll gather the horses up. I'd be better at that than Ames would be." Pap paused and then looked at the gambler. "I take back what I said about you being a pisspot watcher card dealer. You did good here with Slocum."

"Thanks, Pap."

"Better save all our thanks until after we get Hawkins. He ain't going to be this easy the way I have him sized," Slocum said as Pap remounted his horse and then gave them a salute.

"I'll be watching for them," the older man said and rode out of camp.

"Now we wait?" Ames asked.

"Exactly, and waiting ain't fun either," Slocum said, checking on the two bound and gagged rustlers. They were seated in the shadows so they couldn't be seen or warn anyone until it was too late. Satisfied they were secure, Slocum straightened and looked at the fire under the kettle. They would need to keep it stoked up all night so Hawkins wouldn't be suspicious when he rode up.

Slocum certainly wanted his trap to work. Still, Hawkins was no beginner, or stupid. What had they left out? The things undone usually spoiled a trap.

"Can you think of anything we need to do so Hawkins doesn't suspect something's wrong and not come in?" Slocum asked.

"Looks like a perfect setup if we haul this dead man out of sight." Ames lifted one of his arms, waiting for Slocum's assistance.

"Good idea. I'll help you," Slocum said as he took the corpse's other limp arm and they began to tug at the same time. They strained to drag the dead man into the brush, with his spurs plowing the ground, but they quickly had the corpse hidden from sight. Ames even covered the body with a bedroll blanket.

The quarter moon rose and they waited. Pap rode back into camp. Ames got ready to replace him on the night-hawk shift. The mares were settled again, according to the old man.

"Here, you wear the Kid's hat out there." Pap stopped Ames from leaving. "They might recognize that derby of yours even in the dark."

"Good idea," Slocum agreed. "Have some coffee, Pap, and then you pick a place in the trees. And, Ames, don't you take on no army out there. Come back and get us."

"I will," the man said and rode out to herd the horses.

Slocum studied the starlit sea of grass and wondered what the hell was keeping Hawkins. The man was wait-ing till near daylight, when everyone was half-asleep and hardly on their guard. Slocum felt certain it was a planned double-cross on the rustlers. No honor among damn thieves anyway.

He saw the first sign of a line of riders, small dark ants in the distance. By the pearl cast of the night, Slocum could barely make out the half dozen riders lurching in the saddle as they crossed the ridge and headed down the grade for the camp. First he heard the dry coughs of their horses and the muffled sound of hooves on the grass-softened ground, then he heard saddle leather protesting. Someone cleared his throat, and another hissed for him to be quiet.

"Wish Ames was in here," Slocum said under his breath as he knelt at the edge of camp. His right fist was full with the wooden handle of his reloaded Colt, and two more pistols that belonged to the outlaws were ready in his waistband in case Hawkins chose to fight.

"He'll be fine out there unless they split up," Pap said, with the Winchester receiver hard against his cheek, ready to fire.

"He's halted them up there. I think they're fixing to do

just that, split up on us," Slocum said. "Move that way and cover Ames. Our card dealer ain't too knowledgeable yet about this kind of soldiering."

"For a man guarded a pisspot the whole war he ain't bad," Pap said and slipped to the rear to obey Slocum's orders.

The creek's rush over the rocks sounded louder than before. Somewhere in the night an owl hooted several times. Slocum strained his ears to hear whatever Hawkins must be saying to his men. He put the Colt in his other hand and dried his gun hand on the seat of his pants. He listened. Nothing—except the hair on his neck began to rise and he itched in places he hadn't itched in years.

3

The howls and screams of the war party came from out of nowhere in the night. A thunder of hooves meant they were sweeping along the slope toward Hawkins's bunch. Slocum rose and swore under his breath as he tried to make them out better in the starlight. Had they been lying in wait to take the forty or so mares away from Slocum, Pap, and Ames? At any rate, a whole tribe of bucks on horseback were screeching and shooting at Hawkins and his men. Slocum watched in disbelief as the screaming riders swooped in from the east and drove Hawkins's gang over the hill. The outlaws were cussing their horses and firing back sporadically at the attacking Indians.

"What the hell is happening?" Pap asked, raising the rifle to aim.

"Hold your fire. Those Indians are attacking Hawkins. They have to know we are here."

"That's plumb crazy!" Pap said.

"Crazy or not, they've got Hawkins on the run," Slocum said as the running gun battle went over the rise and headed for the military post. "You and I better help Ames corral those mares in the rope pen. Those bucks may come back for the herd when they finish chasing Hawkins's bunch back to Laramie."

33

"Why did they attack him?" Pap asked, scratching his sideburns with his right hand, the Winchester in his left one.

"What kind of Indians were they?" Ames asked, out of breath as slipped from the saddle. "Damn, I thought we'd all lost our hair in this deal."

"We ain't through this day either," Pap said. "Get back on horseback; we got to get them mares up here where they can't steal them with less than a fight. Slocum thinks they'll come back for the horses after they put tail to Hawkins."

"Were they about to jump us?" Ames asked.

"They could have been," Slocum said. "They weren't so far from us that they couldn't have just jumped up and gone to squalling before we knew they were there. You two best go get the horses in here close. I'll watch for them."

"Come on, gambler, we ain't saved our scalps yet," Pap said, untying his own horse.

"There are times your humor is plain grim, Pappy."

"I've been laughing for a long time and aim to go on for many more years." Pap booted his mount from camp and Ames followed.

His partners gone, Slocum turned an ear. He could still hear distant shots being fired. Had that really been Elijah Hawkins's bunch out there? Who were the Indians that attacked in the pitch darkness? He only had a crazy boy's words that Hawkins was the one coming to pay them. A desperate boy's word, too. Slocum grimly considered the thick branch overhead. If the war party didn't turn around and come back in the next hour, it would be full daylight, and they'd need to move out with the horses. That left the living rustlers to deal with.

Slocum knew as well as any man alive the unwritten laws of the West. Any man who stole another's horse faced the same punishment for his crime. Age, deformity, or even mental defectiveness was inexcusable when it came to horse stealing. Horses were the source of their owner's transportation, safety to escape, and livelihood; without them he and his family could perish. Slocum drew a deep breath and went for the rope on his saddle. As he walked in the darkness he could hear Ames and Pap bringing in the herd.

The gunshots over the rise ceased. Slocum undid the leather thong that bound the hemp rope to his saddle and wondered why the Indians had attacked Hawkins's bunch. He quickly scanned the dark slopes to be sure they weren't returning. The harsh texture of the rope felt prickly in his fingers as he began the wraps to make the first noose.

"What kind of Indians were they?" Ames asked as he and Pap dismounted.

"Bloodthirsty to my notion," Pap said, then whirled around to check the still, darkness-shrouded prairie.

"Come dawn," Slocum said, making the rope slide in the knot to lengthen the noose, "I'm riding onto that ridge and seeing how it looks from up there."

"If it's all clear, we make a break for it?" Pap asked.

"We better. If I come riding back hard, you two better be ready to go down fighting."

"I reckon we understand. You'll need two of them neckties," Pap indicated the noose in Slocum's hand.

Ames looked uncomfortable. "We going to use our horses to set them on?" he asked, swallowing hard.

Slocum nodded as he stepped over and undid the lariat on Pap's saddle. His hands steadily fashioned the new knot. Strange, he mused, he himself had cheated the same rope many times. Only an Injun attack would spare the two living rustlers. However, there was nothing out there as the flannel-gray dawn began to open the eye of day.

Long, fiery-orange shafts began to illuminate the rolling land around them.

"Let's get on with it," Slocum said. With the heavy hand of fate on his shoulder, he wanted to think about spring in Alabama. There would be birds singing in the tall oaks and stately walnuts. The smell of rich soil being turned up by a moldboard plow, and red worms wiggling to escape the warm sun. Kildees chasing down the furrows. But that was Alabama, this was Wyoming . . . .

In the full sunlight, Slocum reined the big bay up on the highest point and surveyed the empty prairie. No sign of anyone, Hawkins or the Indians, in any direction. He raised his arm to wave the all clear signal at the others, for them to come on. As he watched for their reply, Slocum could see the condemned rustlers' boots gently swinging back and forth a few feet off the ground as they hung from the cottonwood limb.

In a few minutes the lead mare, a blaze-face sorrel with a long thoroughbred body, splashed through Dead Cow Branch. As if on cue the other mares followed. They were a shinny bunch of mares coming up the grade. Far from the scrubby mustangs that roamed the Wyoming range land, these horses showed the breeding of kings. Some rancher might give Ames's price or even more for them if he was starting a bloodline up there. Slocum checked the land again—nothing.

By evening the mares were back with the grinning farmer. Ira Gustafson came to the door with a bundle in the crook of his arm.

"By Gawd I thank you. She had some troubles and it's fine now. He's a boy! Call him Abraham for the Bible one, huh?"

"By Gawd I'd call him something a damn site better than

Abraham," Pap mumbled to himself and spit to the side.

Slocum swept off his hat as the pale new mother came to the doorway.

"I want to thank you for sending Ira home to help me. I'm so glad you got your horses back," she said.

"Think nothing of it," Slocum said. "Here, take this pistol, Ira. It belonged to a rustler. He won't need it. It'll go good with that twenty-two you got."

The big man accepted the Colt. "I thank you, but they won't steal your mares again."

"They might try," Slocum said and decided to drop the subject.

"We'd invite you in, but . . . we don't have much food . . ." The dirt farmer looked embarrassed over his situation.

"Why, Ira," Ames said, "we'll be back in Fort Laramie in a couple of hours. We can eat there. Thanks anyway." He and Slocum shared a common notion without words; they would not impose on this couple's meager supplies.

They rode back up the valley of the North Platte. To the south a line of bluffs marked the far side of the river. Smoke from hundreds of cooking fires made the air bitter. Wagon train after train huddled on the barren, licked-clean ground. They waited for the final push across the sagebrush-bristled, unforgiving lands of Wyoming, Utah, and Idaho, to reach the promised land—Oregon.

On the mesa beyond, Slocum could make out the white barracks and other buildings that encompassed the fort. Several cavalry patrols rode by them. Finally a buckskin-clad scout reined up and singled out Pap. The older man introduced the scout to the others as Callie Martin.

"Whitcomb, you seen any hostiles today?" Martin asked.

"Why's that?" Pap asked as the other two sat their horses and listened.

"Some damn U.S. senator's man was attacked by a war party about dawn."

"Where at?"

"They thought in the vicinity of Dead Cow Branch, but that was only their general direction because they never crossed the stream."

"What the hell was some senator's man doing off the main trail anyway?" Pap asked.

"Hell, go up and ask him. Got our asses eat out over it by the colonel. Hell, they got half the pony soldiers out riding and looking for the damn hostiles that done it."

"Were they a Sioux war party or what?"

"Funny thing about that, none of them knew." The scout shook his head like he didn't understand half of it. "I can't believe any Injuns attacked a party of armed white men in the darkness."

"Who's the senator?" Slocum asked.

"Senator Tyrone Landers from Ohio. He's the one in charge of all the Indian business in Congress, so the brass at the fort is upset his boy was shot at out here."

"Maybe they were where they didn't belong," Pap said.

"Man, Whitcomb, this is a U.S. senator's son. Christ, he can go where he wants in this country and the Army's supposed to make it safe for him. You know how that goes, man."

"What's his name?" Slocum asked.

"The senator's son is Lamont Landers." Martin turned his horse as if he were late for an appointment and rode off with a "See ya."

Ames nodded and looked wary as the scout rode off. The gambler waited to speak until Martin was beyond hearing his words.

"You thinking what I'm thinking?" Ames asked and Slocum pushed his horse in close.

"Your friend Hawkins has friends in high places, huh?" Slocum said, considering the new turn of events.

"I'm thinking if we'd had some damn shoot-out with them up there, we'd probably had us a congressional incident," Pap said with a look down the road to be sure his friend the scout was gone.

"Also means that this Lamont Landers is in with our old buddy Hawkins, too," Slocum said, not certain of the full implications of such a pact.

"What do you want to do about the mares?" Ames asked. "I'm a gambler, not an Indian fighter. You can have them for twenty dollars, and the name of the man who will buy them."

Slocum considered the man's offer. "I'll let you know in the morning."

"Fine, I'll meet you at the store then," Ames offered. "Thanks for helping me get my mares back. I owe you two."

Both men shook their heads to dismiss the debt. "We come out all right."

Pap and Slocum watched the gambler ride off. They turned their mounts for Pap's place at Squaw Town.

"What the hell is a senator's son doing with that scum?" Pap asked as they headed into camp.

"Those questions I guess are for the Supreme Court to answer and us out here in Wyoming to wonder on," Slocum said. He twisted in the saddle. He spotted her again. The tall Shoshone squaw was riding in the middle of a large party heading out across the prairie. There were several squaws trudging along with many stout paint horses pulling travois loaded with goods and tepees.

They must be going to join their menfolks, Slocum thought, then blinked. There were no men in the group. That was strange. A special home guard always watched after the family groups in all Indian societies that he knew. The camp dogs barked, dashing around the edges. Probably grateful to bark, because before the horse came to these people, the dogs had borne the loads of the camp on small travois.

Were the Shoshone men already out hunting buffalo somewhere? Slocum dismissed the answer to his question as the short Morning Woman stood before him and waited for him to unsaddle. As he undid his girth he could not get over how very handsome the Shoshone woman looked riding the bald-faced horse, whose hide was dark brown as polished walnut. The contrast of the white on the horse's face to his sleek brown coat was as impressive as the full-figured woman in the elkskin-covered saddle.

"Ask Morning Woman if she knows about that tall Shoshone squaw," Slocum directed Pap as his wife scurried about to fetch the horse-watcher boy's hobbles for their horses.

Pap spoke to her in some tongue Slocum did not know. She replied and pointed after her.

"She says she's a medicine woman. Has much power."

"Why is she here?"

Pap asked Morning Woman more in her tongue and then listened for her reply. "To get more food for her people. She is not happy with the goods that they were promised and what really comes."

"Who's fault is that?"

"The Indian Bureau, I'd guess, and those conniving weasels who sell way more out the back door of the warehouse than they give the Indians out in front."

Slocum watched the Shoshone party head northwest across the sweep of the prairie. He had missed her again. He wanted to know more about the tall, alluring woman. Did she have a husband? What was her great medicine that even Pap's Delaware-Fox squaw was impressed with her skills?

Ames would expect his answer on the horse deal by morning. A more important matter for Slocum to consider than a fancy squaw. As the sharp camp smoke found his nose, he watched some of the town's children splashing in the North Platte. Maybe a bath would settle his mind. He'd hike somewhere up or down stream and be alone for a while with his thoughts while he soaked his pores clean.

"Come on, let's go to the sutler's and wash some of this trail dust out of our throats," Pap said, taking him by the sleeve.

The bath could wait.

4

A noisy crowd clustered around a few tables in the back of the sutler's smoke-filled store. Slocum and Pap gave the commotion a long, hard look when they entered. Slocum saw the eye patch and recognized Hawkins among the crowd. Neither Hawkins's obvious contempt nor his apparent cruelty was concealed in the hard look he cast at Slocum, and the faint curl of his upper lip was also unmistakeable. The man's self-serving greed shone like a gold nugget in a new pan. In the cigar smoke and flickering lamplight of the sutler's store, Slocum wondered how their paths had not crossed before.

"What's going on back there?" Pap asked the barkeep while selecting a wine-soaked cheroot from the glass jar.

Slocum picked a fistful of quirlies from the box on the bar. He paid for them then stuck one in the corner of his mouth as he reached in his vest pocket for a match. He struck the lucifer under the bar.

"Lamont Landers," the bartender said. The slight edge of disgust as he spoke was not missed by Slocum as he carefully listened to the man's words. "The Ohio senator's son and some of his friends are drinking champagne to celebrate their victory. Seems they had a close encounter with a band of hostiles early today and they fought them off."

Pap leaned over and lighted his cigar off the flame that Slocum held cupped in hand; he did not believe the bartender's words. Slocum made no move to light his own cigar as he digested the barkeep's speech.

"They routed the Indians?" Slocum asked with a swallow that hurt his throat.

"Yeah, they sent them packing. Guess them bucks took away all their dead like Indians do, because they don't have any scalps, but the figure they give was they killed a dozen or more."

Slocum whipped out the light as flame scorched his fingertips. He stared at Pap. "I thought that scout Martin told us they barely escaped with their hair."

"Makes a lot better newspaper story, don't it? Ohio dude whips the wild savages?" Pap said and struck another match for Slocum to light his small cigar on.

After a deep inhale, Slocum let the smoke roll out his nose. He let the surge of the nicotine relax his mind and muscles. Still struck with disbelief, he intently studied the dark-haired handsome young man with his boot set upon the table. His chest puffed out in his snowy white shirt as he bragged about defeating half the Sioux nation.

A chuckle rose in Slocum's chest as he considered the man's bald-faced lies. Pap elbowed him to cut off his amusement and shoved a glass of whiskey at him. Slocum tossed it down while still gazing at the cluster of noisy men across the room. Landers was going on about the great defense they made while outnumbered by the screaming savages.

Slocum just recalled the tails of their horses in the dim light, headed for the fort's protection, with the war party howling on their butts. Strange none of the white men were shot or hurt. No wounded? They never mentioned who they lost. Hawkins was back there in the crowd, busting his buttons as he added words to verify the younger man's oration. So were his three henchmen, Slocum noted, looking unscathed from the big Injun war as they smugly hung at the edge of the wide-eyed audience of drummers and travelers.

"Quit staring at them and come sit down," Pap said under his breath, steering Slocum by the arm. Before they sat down, they stopped at the appearance of an officer who came through the door.

"Some of you men come out here," the officer said. "We have four corpses we want you to identify if you know the men." The lieutenant looked sharp despite the trail dust on his uniform. Slocum recognized a real soldier under the silver bar. The man was in his forties, old for a career man with such a low rank, but the armistice did that. There were too damn many colonels and captains for a peacetime army. If you wanted to stay in uniform, you took a lower rank. Lots of top sergeants were ex–field officers.

Slocum exchanged a nod with Pap as they finished their first glass of whiskey. They set their glasses down and walked over to see what the officer wanted. Slocum and Pap were the last men out the store. Four dead men were laid out on the ground. The canvas sheets they were wrapped in were open to show their faces.

"These two were hung," the officer pointed with his riding crop. "The two others were shot. We found lots of horse tracks, but we were unable to trail them."

"Hung? What for, Lieutenant?" Hawkins asked. He stood with his hands on his hips like he was some expert. "That man's name's Greenway. The young one is the Kid. I know him from Squaw Town. He arrived here a couple weeks ago. Why they hang him? He's just a boy."

"I suspect," the officer said, tucking his riding crop under his arm, "this execution was done by members of the Anti–Horse Thief Society. I didn't think they were this far west, but obviously they have arrived. These men must have been surprised in camp with stolen horses."

"Any sign of the war party, sir?" Lamont asked, elbowing his way through the onlookers. "They might have done this, and because we discovered them, they attacked us."

"None. Absolutely, this was not the work of hostiles." The officer looked very serious as he spoke. "Besides, Mr. Landers, these war parties always vanish like smoke."

"Then I suggest you call in these chiefs like Red Cloud and explain to them—"

"Mr. Landers," the lieutenant said, snapping his heels together sharply. "You must take your suggestions for any military action to my commanding officer. I am not able to accept such charges from anyone else."

"I will, and we'll bring in these blanket-ass chiefs and tell them to send in those guilty bucks," Landers raged. "There is no way we can ever expect to have a true country for Americans with criminals like that running around attacking white men."

Hawkins obviously saw the futility of his ward saying more about how to operate the western military forces of the United States of America. He herded the speaker and his men back inside the store. Hawkins let the others go in so he could give a hard, final look at Slocum.

Slocum tried to ignore the implications of the glance. Hawkins reminded him of a mastiff dog. Ready to bite with or without an excuse. Mildly, Slocum turned back as someone else spoke to the officer.

"This one is Fonteneu." Indicating the dead horse guard, a French-accented man picked him out. "And that big one is named Oats, Gunter Oats. Mean sumbitch. I see him eat a man's ear off one time in a fight."

"Thank you, gentlemen. Bury them," the officer said to the detail of enlisted men as he wrote in his notebook. He looked hard over at Slocum. "Do you recognize them, sir?"

Slocum shook his head and turned on his heel. Then he stopped, turned back, and asked the officer, "Anti–Horse Thief Society, huh?"

"I figure so. They make those special knots like what we found on those two's necks. Vigilantes and most others just use a lariat and it doesn't break their neck. They strangle, dancing on the end after a long while. This execution was done by folks knew their business." The lieutenant gave a wry shake of his head.

"Thanks, I'll remember that," Slocum said and followed Pap back inside the store.

"You'll remember what?" Pap asked once they were inside and no one was close enough to overhear them. They took their seats at the table.

"How the Anti–Horse Thief Society makes those certain knots when they hang rustlers."

Pap cleared his throat and spat on the floor beside his chair. "Little sawed-off Yankee know-it-all sumbitch. It was heel-snapping little bastards like him why I hated scouting for them blue bellies."

"That man is a good officer." Slocum grinned over his glass of whiskey. "Like him or not."

"Why? 'Cause he thinks it's an Anti–Horse Stealing knot that you learned in the Army of the Confederacy?"

"Noncoms never did appreciate a good officer." Slocum wanted to laugh at Pap's show of anger.

"I knew one."

"Who the hell was that?"

"A Captain Logan."

Slocum didn't answer the man. He wondered what Hawkins would try if he and Pap bought Ames's horses.

There was a matter of some eight hundred dollars Slocum didn't have, to pay Ames for them, that looked like a mountain they'd have a hard time crossing. The card games he'd seen in the store were for two bits. Too far from payday at the fort to make a killing big enough to pay for the mares. The eight hundred dollars profit they'd bring up on the Wind River would winter him, Pap, and Pap's squaw somewhere up in the mountains. Still time to ride south before the geese flew, to let the desert sun warm his sore muscles and some señorita rub away the stiffness in his back.

"Don't look now, but that braggart boy is coming over here," Pap said.

"Lamont Landers of Canton, Ohio," he said openly. Slocum had seen his kind in the East.

"John Slocum," he said and rose, not offering to shake his hand. "Pap Whitcomb here."

"Well, you sound very Southern."

"Is that against the law?" Slocum asked.

"No, I just wondered what area? My father served with the occupational forces after the war in the South."

"Van Buren, Arkansas?" Slocum lied.

"No, he was in Georgia and Alabama."

"I was across from the Indian nation, right on the Arkansas River," Slocum said and started to sit down with a nod of curt good-bye.

"Yes, nice to meet you, Slocum and Whitcomb. I'm with the Indian Bureau here now. I'm seeing how things should be handled out west. I think with a few good soldiers and some men like yourself that know how to fight, this Indian matter can be put to rest in no time."

"Maybe," Slocum said.

"I know a few of you Rebs could whip these miserable blanket-ass wretches, couldn't you?" Lamont asked, directly challenging Slocum.

"Why, Mr. Landers, I ain't seen a Reb in so long I don't think there are any more left."

Lamont chose to laugh at those words. He slapped his knee and had a hard time controlling himself. "There are some—Oh my—Yes, that is funny, but mark my words there are lots of them out here. Real Rebs, too."

5

The morning sun cut across the valley of the North Platte. The golden rays gilded the sea of canvas wagon tops. Oxen protested in deep-throated cries as they were driven off to graze in distant pastures. Dull herders, boys in overalls, wearing shapeless felt hats or woolen caps, drove them afoot. The dust cloud from the cloven hooves rose up to the boys' knees. They cracked whips and cursed the dull animals unwilling to more than shuffle. Slocum wondered if their Baptist mothers back in camp would scour their tongues yellow with lye soap if they ever heard the profane words the boys spent on the bovines.

"I never figured he'd take our offer," Pap said, then spit tobacco sideways into the road dust as they headed eastward.

"He admitted he's a gambler," Slocum said as they passed an Indian woman with a short, stout pony hooked to travois poles. Slocum studied her for a moment. Silver coins on a necklace glistened on top of her molded breasts encased by a yellow buckskin blouse. Slocum twisted in the saddle to appreciate her form and the movement of her hips under the leather skirt. Her raven-black hair was done in braids and shone in the morning light. She did not look Slocum's way as she led the fat spotted pony on. The hiss of the poles in the dust sounded loud mixed with the other noises, of mules braying and roosters crowing.

"You were saying?" Pap asked.

"Ames isn't a fool. He knew the only men that he could hire would easily be bought off or frightened by Hawkins and his gang. Ames didn't have much choice but to let us have the mares and hope we live to pay him back."

"Didn't he say Hawkins threatened to kill him if he sold us the mares?"

"That's the chance that Ames takes. But he isn't a man without guts; he just knows when he's whipped. Driving the herd three hundred miles up in the Wind River is beyond his ability."

"I can't figure why he ain't going along with us if he's so damn worried about his investment."

"I think he's weighed our chances of making it alive and figures they are about as good as drawing to an inside straight, so he's bowed out."

"What are them odds?" Pap asked.

"Tell me one out of fifty two."

"Damn, we ain't very well off then." Pap laughed as if the notion struck his funny bone. "So we head out for the Wind River next."

"It's working so far. Ames is going to stay close to the sutler's post store and not let them suspect anything is going on."

"Hell, Hawkins knows by now we're headed up the valley. He's got more snitches than the devil himself."

"He might figure that we're just a draw and when he follows us, Ames will move the mares. Besides, Hawkins doesn't know that we slipped your woman and them pack mules out of Squaw Town last night. They're going to meet us midday, and then we're taking these mares on a fast trip to west of Cheyenne over the mountains and not resting them until we're across the Laramie River."

"That's a fur piece of country to cover."

"If he follows us that far, we'll know how serious Hawkins is about taking the mares from us."

Pap spit again, then wiped his mouth on his sleeve. "And this rancher Billings who's supposed to buy them. I figured that Ames never would tell you his name last night."

"What the hell good was our taking them up there for him, if we didn't have the buyer's name?"

"Ames held that like a hole card even if he did spill his beans on the whole horse deal to every scallywag in the damn fort looking for help."

"Here's where we turn and ride out to the sodbuster's," Slocum said. "You see anyone coming up our backtrail?"

"Nope, but that don't mean nothing."

"I know," Slocum admitted. "I just hoped if he sent some flunky to follow us it would be obvious as all get out."

Pap grinned open his whisker-fringed toothless gap of a mouth. "It ain't going to be that easy, Slocum. Ain't nothing that simple when you're dealing with a badger like Hawkins."

"Pap, somehow I knew it, but you can always hope," Slocum said. "Let's lope our horses and get there."

He cast one last look across the sea of parked wagons and rigs. Somewhere out there a man, his wife, and family were getting ready to go plant fruit trees in Oregon ashes. Slocum had seen it for himself. Somehow the pale Oregon dust from some long ago volcanic eruption made a perfect medium to grow the like. With water diverted from some source to satisfy the roots' thirst, the tree would soon shade the earth and bear barrels of crisp apples each year. Slocum wished he had that man's problems instead of wondering about a one-eyed pirate who would back-shoot his own brother for a gold coin. And how did the senator's son fit in Hawkins's plans? That braggart was another key to benefit Hawkins's purposes.

When they rode up, Gustafson was setting fence posts and waved. His young wife emerged from the soddy with a bundle of blankets in her arms that was no doubt the new baby. The smile of pride seemed indelible on her fresh face.

"Morning," Slocum said with a tip of his hat for the missus. "We've come to move the mares."

"They're up on top grazing. They've had a good drink this morning," the farmer said, wiping the sweat from his face on his brawny suntanned arm.

"I have your final payment and a note from Ames for you to release the mares to us," Slocum said. The man quickly pocketed the small purse of money and shook his head as he read the paper.

"No problem," the big man said. "He'd not have any horses were it not for you two."

"I want you to tell anyone that asks," Slocum said as his horse shifted under him and he checked him, "that Pap and I are taking them to the Wind River country."

"That's where you're really going?" A cloud of doubt spread over the big man's face as if he could not believe Slocum's words.

"Yes, we're going there. But I don't want them to hurt you or the missus for that information, because Pap and I can handle them if they try to get us."

"I'll be telling them to go to hell."

"No! That's not the way I want it," Slocum insisted, jerking on the bits to settle his sidestepping horse.

"Good then," Gustafson said, "we'll tell them you went to the Wind River." The farmer crossed his great arms over his burly chest as if the notion did not set well, but he would obey the request.

Slocum looked at the couple hard until both nodded in agreement. He envied the big man, not for his poor choice of thin prairie land, but for the woman who always seemed so fresh, so happy. The soddy must be warm shelter from the elements and their marriage bed a source of excitement and pleasure.

"Ma'am," he said. "Good day, and you, too, Gustafson. May you do well here."

"We shall," the big man said, taking possession of his wife and child under one arm. The confidence the farmer exuded was obvious, and Slocum touched his hat good-bye as he and Pap went for the horse herd.

Pap circled them and Slocum took the near side. After a few whistles to gain their attention, the herd raised their heads like they understood the way was northwest across the long, flat mesa. Slocum felt grateful for their trail-broken nature and raised his left arm to direct them as a group.

He turned in the saddle to wave a last time at the farmer and his bride and baby. He and Pap were Wind River bound.

The horses moved like swift fire. Their legs stiffened as they came thundering off the steep hillside, then churned up dust as they rose from the next arroyo to climb atop still another long, grassy mesa.

"Morning Woman." Pap pointed proudly to the distant dot.

"You'll be glad she's along," Slocum said as they trailed the mares in a long trot.

"She's a good one," Pap said.

"A man can use all the good ones there are," Slocum agreed. The acrid dust was scorching his nostrils. He could use the kerchief around his neck to mask out the bitterness, but the occasional fresh wind out of the south was more comforting than the hot mask would be.

"Ever had you an Injun woman?" Pap asked.

"I've known a few," Slocum said, recalling the Shoshone woman from Squaw Town. He would have liked to spend an entire winter in her lodge. Be a fat chance of that happening. He twisted in the saddle and squinted at the horizon. Survival had taught him to keep his eyes open, and he always periodically checked the country he rode through. Being observant had been his hole card for living so long. He settled in the saddle; nothing in sight.

"I don't think they're on to us. You and Morning Woman keep the mares headed northwest. I'm going to find a place to take a bath," Slocum said.

"There's a creek called Witcherson north a couple miles," Pap said.

"Glad you know this country." Slocum smiled at his partner. "I don't figure you'll have a problem here."

"No. These mares trail like camp dogs. But you'll probably catch pneumonia taking a dang bath." Pap shook his head in disapproval. "Worse than a damn Sioux squaw I had once. She was always going swimming. Don't say I didn't warn you either!"

"She die from pneumonia?"

"Hell no, she run off with Frenchie Devereu."

"What for?" Slocum asked.

"Guess Frenchie had a bigger one than mine. No. But he had a set of painted ponies she couldn't quit looking at all day. I'd seen that look before. Why I knew she'd run off with him. Big powerful paint horses stole that fickle witch's heart."

"He pay you for her?"

"Hell no, but I had the last laugh."

"How was that?" Slocum asked.

"A couple moons later, she stole them paints and left that old Frenchie drunk on his ass."

"Where did she go then?"

"Back to Sitting Bull, I guess, never heard of her again. But that Frenchie was sure mad when I seen him up at Bannock leading a pissy-tailed bunch of Injun ponies for a pack string. Served him right, though, for taking her from me."

Slocum saluted the grinning Morning Woman when she rode up with the two pack mules. Then he turned his horse off for Witcherson Creek beyond the northern horizon.

Sunlight danced like cold coins on the rushing stream. Slocum wondered as he rode up if what he saw standing in the rushing water was real or a mirage. Naked as Eve, she neither turned away nor seemed upset about his discovery of her bathing. He drew up the horse and blinked his eyes. She was real enough all right. The same woman he had seen in Squaw Town, the tall Shoshone from Fort Laramie. The short hair on the nape of his neck stiffened. Slocum twisted in the saddle to search around for any sign of a trap. This had to be an ambush. Or a way to rush Pappy and Morning Woman while he was gone. She'd keep him occupied, so her bunch could swoop down and steal the brood mares.

Damn, this was serious. He'd been so damn busy worrying about Hawkins, he'd forgot about the Indians wanting horses. They lived and breathed ownership. Horses were their wealth.

A smile formed in the corner of her dark brown lips. He was forced to stand up in the stirrups and search around some more. Filled with dread and indecision, Slocum tried to measure his vulnerability at the moment. He studied the rustling cottonwoods that lined the bank, expecting any moment the shrill war cries of some bloodthirsty bucks with war-painted faces, lips drawn tight over their teeth, and death in raised hands—gun, knife, or tomahawk.

Hearing nothing but the rising wind, Slocum settled in the saddle and slowly turned back to contemplate her.

He could see how taut her breasts were as she waded toward him. Capped with dark nipples, they pointed up like peaks. He found her presence in this isolated stretch of water hard to comprehend. Slocum drew a deep breath filled with the uncertainty of the moment. Her flat stomach dimpled with a navel above the dark patch of hair that he could hardly take his stare away from.

"You took a long time to get here," she said.

"Hell, lady, if I'd known you were here like this, I'd've come days sooner," he said and turned to check again for any signs of a possible ambush. "You sure you ain't got me confused with someone else?"

She folded her arms over her treasures. "You are Slow—come?"

"Yes, that's who I am." He frowned, wondering how the hell she knew his name. Still he fretted over the notion she might be the bait to get him killed. "How the hell did you know I was coming here?"

"The great bird told me two moons ago you would pass here with an old man and a band of mares."

"You're saying an eagle told you that?" He was certain at this point he understood her problem. She quite simply was out of her mind. He'd known women before that were sort of mentally unbalanced. Damn shame for someone as good-looking as her.

"Yes, they told me then you were with a woman had red hair," she said.

"Oh Jesus," Slocum swore and narrowed his eyelids to look at her even harder. "You say eagles told you that?"

Over a month before, he'd been in central Nebraska, at Shasha Carnes's homestead. Shasha lived in a soddy, where Slocum had spent considerable time and effort to console the poor distraught widow.

Actually he'd brought her husband's last effects to her. Slocum had to inform the lovely red-maned widow that her husband was dead; shot in an ambush down in the Indian Nation by some mangy dogs. Before Slocum rode up to her place, he had tracked the back-shooters down and killed them to settle the debt.

However, the consoling business required ten days, and the two of them blame near wore out the springs in her steel-frame bed, the only decent piece of furniture she owned. Then he'd put Shasha on the stage for Omaha, so she could go find her aunt who ran a gambling hall.

How did this Indian woman know about all of that?

"What's your name?" he asked, half-riled at her knowledge.

"My name is Blue Feather. You did come to take a bath here?" she asked, standing only a few feet from the bank.

He dismounted and threw his hat down. "I damn sure did, and I don't believe in witches either."

"I am not witches. My name is Blue Feather."

"Only witches talk to eagles," he said, struggling to stand up and pull one boot off at the same time. He hopped around, and finally, in a great rush of air, his foot escaped the leather confines. The notion of holding her shapely body in his arms had him stirring with need.

"You some kind of a medicine woman?" he asked, glaring at her with one boot off, one boot on.

"Yes, Blue Feather has much medicine. My spirits are very strong."

"The hell with the spirits. If I get this damn boot off, we'll see what kinda strong smoke you and I can make together." He hobbled around on one stocking foot in a tight circle until finally he was out of breath from tugging, and in the end the other boot came free. He threw it down. Next he took off his holster, set the gun where he could grab it if necessary, then throwing caution to the wind, he removed his vest, shirt, and britches. With a deep inhale, he paused for a long moment and glared at her. She was too damn good to be true. Hell with it! He shed his one-piece underwear, then plowed into the stream.

The water on his legs felt ice cold. While the chill caught his breath, it did not diminish his desire as he waded across the sandy bottom to be closer to her.

She held her finger to her lips to silence him. Slocum shook his head in disbelief as he admired the ripe figure before him. His breathing became harder. As if on cue, she moved inside his outstretched arms and pressed her body to his. He kissed and hugged her. The heat of her supple, muscular form against his chest filled him with the need to possess her.

"Let's go to the shore," he said.

"Yes," she said softly and then kissed him very hard on the mouth. Her long fingers held his face to her hungry mouth as her tongue sought his. Apart at last, they laughed with excitement as they splashed out of the stream.

On the bank, she tossed a colorful trade blanket into the wind to open it and then spread it over the short buffalo grass. Blue Feather knelt on the blanket before him.

Was it a trap? Too damn bad! At the moment, he'd have rather died making love to her than anything he could think of. Slocum dropped to his knees to face her. For a long moment he could not believe his good fortune. They swiftly meshed into each other's arms.

Her long, dark lashes shut, and the soft sighs from her parted lips increased his own urgency as he felt her breasts.

On top of her, he moved between her long legs. Her limbs quickly parted for him, and they soon shared each other's body in a flight to match an eagle's soaring. Above them the cottonwood leaves rustled and the wind whispered over their fierce passion.

Then in a final drive and an explosion that drained away the fire consuming them, they dissolved into an intimate pile of flesh against flesh.

"Blue Feather, maybe you've got eagles that talk to you. That tell you things. But I'm a man of the real world," Slocum said, his head propped on his hand and elbow so he could admire her beauty. "You ain't got some bucks going to steal our horses while I'm up here lying with you?"

"No!" She looked at him as if shocked he'd even think such a thing. "Blue Feather needs Slow-come's help. The whiskey men soon come back."

"The what?" he asked.

"The whiskey men come to my reservation. Sell plenty bad stuff to my people. You must stop them."

"Did you talk to the Indian agent about this?" he asked. Simple enough, the agent would stop it. Selling booze to Indians was against the law on any reservation.

She shook her head. "He no help."

"How many whiskey sellers are there?" Slocum could hardly believe her words about the authorities. Stopping the sale of spirits was the agent's job.

Blue Feather held up her fingers.

"Four of them?"

"Yes, that many."

"Say, pretty gal, I don't know about this business of me stopping that many whiskey runners that the agency can't do nothing about. I can't fight four guys. Besides Pap and me got business up north. We've got to deliver these horses to collect our money. Those mares are all the worldly goods I've got right now."

"I can pay you," she said, starting to get up.

"Hold it. Pay me what?" he asked, nearly amused at the notion. Slocum held her down with his free arm so she didn't leave him. What did she mean about paying him anyway? Indians didn't have money.

"I can pay you in gold," she said, settling herself down beside him again. Her fingertip reached out to tease the fine hairs on his chest.

"Gold, huh?" He almost shuddered with excitement as she continued to trace on his breastbone with her fingernail.

"Yes, with enough gold you can hire more men to help you stop them," she said softly.

"How did you figure all this out?" he asked.

Blue Feather smiled as she raised herself up to sprawl her treasures on top of his chest. Snake-like, her palm slithered down his rock-hard stomach in search of his source. Her actions quickened his breathing.

"No more talk," she said. "I think there is more of you left, Slow-come."

"What if we can't—" His words were taken away as her fingers began to arouse him. Slocum raised his head up and kissed her hard. His heart was running away as she sat up and straddled his hips. A gleam of mischief turned up the corners of her mouth as she reached under and with a firm grasp guided him inside her ring. Later there would be time to figure out this whiskey business. Slocum grinned as Blue Feather cried out in pleasure each time she raised and lowered herself on his turgid shaft. What an ambush.

6

Pap shook his head in disbelief. "My gods, man, you went off for a bath and all you could find was that good-looking tall Shoshone woman?" He cast another quick look at Blue Feather.

Slocum smiled. "That's all I could find."

"Maybe bathing ain't so bad after all." Pap slapped his saddle horn. "I was halfway expecting you to catch a cold. Why, Billy be damn, she's better than catching an arm-long trout out of the Wind River."

"She has some problems. Tells me that whiskey peddlers are ruining her tribe with their bad whiskey."

"The only kind they ever sell Injuns anymore is bad whiskey. In the old days, they'd got killed selling such piss-poor stuff to them red devils, but now the Injuns can't fight nor complain since it's illegal to buy the stuff. What's she wanting us to do?"

"To stop them."

"Hell, why us? Why can't the Shoshone Injun agent to do that?" Pap gave Slocum a hard look as they rode behind the horse herd.

"I tried that on her. He either can't or else he's in cahoots with the whiskey sellers."

"He probably makes a share of the sales. Them Injun

agents are all too crooked to fit in a coffin. They screw them in the ground when one dies."

"Hold up! Aren't those Indians out there?" Slocum squinted to make out the figures on the rise. They were warriors all right. Horse-stealing young bucks were all he needed to go along with Hawkins's threat.

"Looks like a scouting party," Pap said as both men jerked out their Winchesters in preparation.

"No!" Blue Feather cried out, seeing what they were doing. She booted her horse in close to stop them from taking any action. "Those are more squaws from my tribe."

"They damn sure look like bucks to me," Pap said.

Slocum wondered, too.

"Wait, I will get them," she said.

Blue Feather loped her powerful horse out to greet them. As Slocum watched her ride off over the prairie, he wondered, Had she set him up? Just in case—he levered a shell in the chamber of the oily-smelling long gun. Friend or foe. Damn, they had enough problems with Hawkins, they didn't need Indian ones. But with the Plains Indians as upset as they were over the takeover of the Black Hills, anything could and probably would happen. Those mountains were the homes of their gods—like taking some church from the preacher who owned it so they could tear it up looking for gold. The federal government would never do that—but they took the Black Hills from the Sioux, crowding the buffalo eaters westward in the Green River country north of them, certainly not too far away for raiding parties.

"By God, they're women," Pap said.

Slocum took the shell out and eased the chamber closed. Still wary, he watched them approach. He finally stuck the Winchester in the boot and loped out for an explanation.

There were five Indian women on horseback with Blue Feather. They were dressed in men's clothing, and their bare brown legs straddled war saddles. They carried arms—rifles and pistols—on their persons.

"Who are they?" Slocum asked.

"These are part of the war party that ran off the horse stealers," Blue Feather said.

Slocum studied the matter for a moment. "The war party that ran Hawkins off that night?"

"Yes, the others will soon come," she said. "We have been scattered so the Army could not find us."

"You knew those men were going to attack us?" Slocum asked, looking at the women's smug faces as they sat their mounts. Though they probably were not able to understand his English completely, they obviously knew why he was acting so shocked.

Blue Feather said something to her warriors, and they laughed. Some covered their mouths with their hands to contain the hilarity, their dark eyes stealing looks at Slocum.

"I told them you believed that Shoshone women were fierce warriors."

"Yes, tell them I believe they are. Were any killed or wounded?"

She shook her head. "We fired our old guns in the air. They ran like sheep, huh?"

"Why women warriors?"

"The agent makes the men come every other day and be counted. He does not count women; I think he does not worry women will fight."

"Why did you protect us?"

"We want you to help us stop the whiskey sellers."

"Can't your women do that?"

Blue Feather pursed her lips as if she were thinking how to answer him. Then she shook her head. "No, we have tried."

"Pap and I owe you one, so I reckon we'll try to stop

them for you." Slocum wasn't certain of anything at the moment.

"Good." She smiled warmly and they rode back to the herd.

A woman spoke up in Shoshone, and Blue Feather listened, nodding as the woman continued to explain something. Blue Feather finally rode back to join Slocum.

"What is wrong?" he asked her.

"There are men coming after you. These women were near their camp last night, and the men say they are coming to take these horses away from you."

"I thought so," Slocum said. "How many are there?"

She held up four fingers.

Slocum nodded his understanding. He rose in the stirrups and turned, contemplating who was pursuing them and when they'd try to jump them. There was no need for the rustlers to be in a hurry; he and Pap were moving the horse herd in the direction they needed to go.

"What did we do to deserve all these women?" Pap asked as Slocum and the Shoshone woman caught up with the man and the herd.

"Meet the Shoshone warriors that sent Hawkins's bunch running for their lives the other night." Slocum gestured to the women on horseback around them.

"They did that?" Pap blinked his eyes in disbelief.

"Them and a few more. They also say we've got company on our tail."

"That's nice to know, huh?"

"Real nice."

"What we aim to do about our tail?"

"I'd like to send them packing. Maybe sneak up tonight and do that," Slocum said, considering his options. "They could trail us to the Wind River. After we do all the hard work, they could take the damn mares away from us up there."

"I say we send them back to Hawkins. You and me?"

"No, not this time. You better watch the herd and I'll take some of Blue Feather's women-bucks here." Slocum gave a head toss to mean the women riding with them, and Blue Feather gave her consent.

"It damn sure ain't nice what a squaw does to a man," Pap said and reined his horse after the herd.

"You mad?" Slocum shouted after him.

Pap turned sideways across his saddle. "What for?"

"How they might handle them horse rustlers on our tail?"

Pap spit off at a bed of pancake cactus. "Hell no, them no-accounts aiming to ambush us deserve whatever these Injun gals got in mind for them."

"Good, we're thinking alike then," Slocum said.

"How many should go?" Blue Feather asked.

"Four of us should be enough." He looked to the Shoshone woman for an answer.

"Yes."

"Good, we'll go after sundown," Slocum said and returned her wink.

The coyotes were yipping. Darkness cloaked the plains as Slocum, Blue Feather, and two other women mounted their horses. The starlight sparkled on the small band of mares and saddle horses on the prairie when Slocum looked back at them.

One-who-runs, the scout, took the lead. She leapt on her horse as if she had springs in her legs. Slocum thought the fourth member who joined them was the oldest of the warrior women. Blue Feather called her Beads, short for the silver beads she wore except when she was at war. Their faces were painted black. Blue Feather had used the waxy black paint to cover Slocum's white skin, too, and the backs of his hands. They had taken only dark horses without white markings to ride. At times as they rode, Slocum marveled at the women's ability to disappear in the starlit night even though he knew by the muffled bare hooves that they were around him.

After several hours' ride, the scout halted them. Slocum saw the distant light of a camp fire and could hear the men's crude talking carrying down the arroyo.

"We must take the horses back," Blue Feather whispered to him, "or theirs will smell them and call."

They slipped to the ground, muzzling their mounts so they did not nicker as they led them away. Slocum glanced over his shoulder into the curtain of night and wondered who was in the camp as the four of them headed behind the mesa under the starry sky.

The horses were finally hobbled and secure in a draw; they set out afoot for the camp. From the ridge, Slocum and the women paused on their bellies to study the camp. A night owl scolded them as he swooped low over the ground in search of a meal. Slocum saw that some of the men were already in their bedrolls. The fire was rather large. He decided that they must have brought wood with them to make such a blaze. Slocum knew that cow chips never did that much for lighting up the night.

"What's next?" he whispered to Blue Feather beside him on the ground.

"Beads will get their horses, while One-who-runs will draw off the guard."

"That's dangerous, ain't it?" Slocum asked.

"Men are fools for women," she said very confidently.

"Yes, even me," he said grimly. Blue Feather glanced at him and gave him a disapproving head shake.

He watched One-who-runs slip like an elusive shadow in the night. One moment he saw her, and then she was gone from his vision, only to reappear when his eyes adjusted again. He could see the zigzag pattern on the blanket that she wore over her shoulders.

Slocum rolled on his side and drew the Colt as she neared the camp. He watched the red light of the fire find her like a precious stone in the glare. The distance was too far for a handgun, but he hoped that if anything went wrong, he would be able to do something to help her.

He noticed the night guard rise to his feet and look around warily as she stepped into the full firelight before him.

"Time for us to go," Blue Feather said to him. "He is distracted."

"Yes," Slocum agreed, seeing One-who-runs slip the blanket off her shoulders and expose herself to the tall guard. The rich copper of her bare body glistened in the fire's light.

In a half crouch and run, Slocum followed Blue Feather. He hoped his boots were as quiet as her knee-high moccasins and the whisper of fringe as she moved fluidly toward the camp.

Could One-who-runs handle the tall guard? Slocum wondered as they approached the sleeping forms. Blue Feather drew her knife and Slocum followed suit. From the rear, like smoke, Beads joined them and they nodded as each one chose a sleeping rustler to kneel beside.

"You make one squawk, this knife will cut your throat," Slocum whispered in the man's ear.

There were grunts, but nothing more from the other two as Blue Feather and Beads were over them with their knives ready. Bedclothes were stripped back, and quickly the would-be rustlers were facedown with their hands bound in rawhide laces behind them.

Slocum straightened and looked around for One-who-runs. The guard in the fire's light was on his belly, with Beads tying his hands behind his back.

"What's them gawdamn squaws going to do to us?" one man grunted. "That you, Slocum? Hell, I know it is."

"They'll probably cut our balls off," another said, "if we're lucky."

"Dammit, shut up! Don't give them no gawdamn ideas."

"They don't speak English."

"I do," Slocum said, tossing his knife in the air and catching it by the handle as he squatted among the trussed-up men. "I want some damn quick answers."

"Go to hell!"

"Blue Feather!" Slocum shouted. "Come give this mouthy one a haircut."

She spoke to One-who-runs. In a bound, the woman was standing over the crying man and had a fistful of his hair wrapped around her fingers. She hacked it off under her fist as he screamed at her to quit.

"Now, we know these women can scalp you or castrate you without any assistance. I want some answers and quickly."

"What you going to do to us?"

"Never mind. You better talk up or you're going to be the first one gelded and the next one can answer the question." Slocum looked around. His threat had silenced their tough mouths.

"You know what we're doing here," the guard said.

"No, I don't."

"Hawkins sent us out here to get them mares. He wanted us to take them away from you before you got to the Wind River."

"Guess you made a big mistake."

"How's that?" one of the others said.

"For working for someone dumb like Hawkins in the first place."

The women were clearing the camp. They hustled about gathering the men's clothing articles, blankets, saddles, food stocks, guns, and boots. The items were bound in great mounds that they tied up in blankets to carry off.

"You going to let us live?" one of the men asked in a low tone.

"That's up to them," Slocum said and stretched his stiff back muscles as he rose to his feet.

Blue Feather drew him aside. Slocum waited for her to speak.

"We could do many things to these men, but they are your enemies," she said. "What do you wish we do?"

"I can't say I want them killed or cut up too bad. Going home barefooted and in their underwear is very humiliating."

"Hum . . . what?" she asked.

"A loss of face. To be disgraced. Feel very lowly like a snake."

"Why not give then an X on their face to remember this by?" she asked.

"Your party," Slocum said.

She turned and spoke to the women. The others nodded in understanding. Slocum watched the two women jerk one of the man to his knees. One-who-runs held him up by the hair on his head while Beads used her knife on his face. His shrill cries of protest carried across the plains. Slocum saw the small dark X bleeding on his cheek before the women dropped him.

"This man you speak of, Hawks?" Blue Feather asked. "He is the one who brings the skinny cattle for our meat and sells my people the bad whiskey. If he was here, they would have tortured him."

"I understand. We share the same enemy," Slocum said.

After they completed marking the men, Slocum considered the men. The squaws rushed about to ready the outlaws' horses to pack all the things they had gathered.

"You better say the Sioux did this to you," Slocum said. "You better make the lie very strong. Any man says three Indian women jumped him and used him for whatever they wanted to do and stole all their personal goods will be the laughing stock of Fort Laramie. You understand?"

There were no words from the four men belly-down in the stripped camp. The fire was down to ashes as the coyotes welcomed the new sliver of a rising moon. Slocum touched his hat and then swung on the horse that Beads had brought up for him to ride back. "You fellows have a nice walk back."

Slocum heard the words as the horse under him hopped up the bank. "Screw you, Slocum, you sumbitch!"

The dawn came early for Slocum. Only a few hours' sleep and it was time to roll on. Satisfied the pursuers would be no further problem to them, his bunch could easily reach the Laramie River without problems, unless Hawkins telegraphed to Cheyenne for more of his help to stop them. That was just a chance they took, and he shrugged it away.

The sagebrush camp fire carried the heavy smell of fresh coffee as he swept off the blanket holding in his body heat. He didn't know when Blue Feather had risen from the bedroll beside him. She was not in sight. Slocum recalled how weary they had been from the night's journey, and the crowd they slept among had kept them from becoming intimate when they returned.

Slocum felt pleased as he stretched. With sleep-numbed fingers he buttoned his shirt. They had several days to move west before those men of Hawkins's shuffled into civilization and Hawkins realized he'd been denied the horse herd.

"Morning, Pap," he said, pouring coffee from the granite pot.

"Guess you got them scallywags?" Pap asked, sitting cross-legged with a tin plate of flapjacks in his lap.

"Yes, they are going home this morning in their underwear, barefooted and with large X's cut in their left cheeks so they're marked and we can tell them."

"My gawd, I can't hardly believe you sent them home barefooted and in their underwear." Pap shook his head in disbelief and forked another piece of pancake in his mouth.

"They won't forget last night for a long time."

"What's next?"

"I want you to ride into Cheyenne and buy us a good fifty-caliber Sharps rifle and a hundred rounds of ammunition."

Pap paused in his eating and looked hard at Slocum. "We going hide hunting somewheres?"

"No, but I thought last night as I laid up on that rim while One-who-runs charmed that guard—if I'd had a Sharps like that, I could have eliminated him."

"I'm more partial to sending them back barefooted and without their clothes." Pap shook his head in disbelief and amusement. "They were damn lucky them squaws didn't cut everything clean off even with their damn bellies."

"They knew it, too. Oh, in case you wanted to know, they said Hawkins sent them out after us."

"Figured so."

"And Hawkins is the guy selling the Shoshone bad whiskey and sorry beef."

"He must have a train full of bad tricks."

Slocum stopped, struck by the notion of Hawkins doing

something like that. "He may use the train to get there ahead of us and try to stop us."

"How did you figure that out?"

"Just a notion. You saddle up and go buy that Sharps. We'll meet you west somewhere on the road."

"I'll find you. I may be getting old, but I can still trail a titmouse up a bluff."

Slocum agreed and took the plate of pancakes Morning Woman gave him. He looked about, but the Shoshone women were not in sight.

"Where did my warriors go?" he asked, taken aback by his discovery.

"Rode out about daybreak. Told Morning Woman something and then left."

"Ask her what they plan to do," Slocum said, upset over the notion.

Pap spoke to the woman in her tongue. She said something, then she busied herself breaking up their camp so she could repack the two mules and be ready to leave.

"Morning Woman says they will meet us later."

"Oh," Slocum said, wondering what the leggy medicine woman would do next. Hell, him and Pap had horses to move, no need to worry about her. She was a big girl. He wiped the syrup from the corners of his mouth with his kerchief and thought again about her long, silky legs wrapped around him. The notion forced him to grin.

7

Throughout the day, Morning Woman led her heavily loaded pack mules with enough impatience to make them jog close behind her pony. A small cloud of dust was churned up by the herd of mares as Slocum kept them moving. To the north and parallel to their pathway, the Union Pacific train tracks struck a course through the mountain peaks that lined the horizon. Slocum also knew that back to the northeast lay the sprawling center of commerce Cheyenne, which they'd purposely circled south to avoid.

As the day dragged into afternoon, he wished that Pap would hurry and catch up with them. Slocum planned to push over the mountains the next day and down to the Laramie River, where he could rest the mares on the ranch of a couple he knew. However, without Pap to help him hurry the laggards along, such a drive would be impossible. He and the Indian woman would be three days making the same distance.

A few days of the Laramie River country's rich grass and sweet water in their bellies and the mares would be rested for the last hundred-or-so-mile drive on to the Wind River. Road-weary, Slocum slouched in the saddle and drew a deep breath. Be good to have the responsibility of the horse herd over with. One thing that kept creeping into his thoughts all day as he herded the horses was that Elijah Hawkins wouldn't take the loss of this herd's profit in good faith.

At sundown, Slocum made a rope corral around some scrub pines and put the mares inside. Earlier he'd watered them in a branch of water so they'd be fine for the night. He wished they were already on the Laramie. Another camp to make, he wiped the sweat off his forehead with his sleeve and started back to help Morning Woman. Slocum was counting the time until—

The mule screamed and half reared on the end of Morning Woman's lead rope as the report of a large-caliber rifle went over their heads. The mule had been struck in the neck, and blood quickly spurted from the large wound as the injured animal settled on his weakened hind legs and then fell over sideways, jerking the lead rope from the stunned woman's hands.

"Goddammit get down!" Slocum shouted to Morning Woman as she looked around for the shooter and tugged on the other mule's lead. With his Colt cocked and ready in his hand, Slocum rushed to her aid. In long strides, his boot heels barely struck the ground as he leapt over low bushes. He burst across the last stretch of open ground. His primary goal was to get her out of harm's way. Why didn't she get down? She acted as if she were too shocked by the shooting to obey him.

Slocum understood the senselessness of his firing at a faraway marksman who had barely missed smashing down Morning Woman.

The wounded mule thrashed on his side when Slocum reached the woman; the packs had been spilled open by the fall. Slocum caught Morning Woman by the waist in a flying tackle and literally flung both of them behind the downed mule's back. A sharp spray of dust from another heavy bullet struck the ground close by and stung their faces in their plunge to safety. The thunderous roll of the muzzle blast upset the mares in the trap. They whined anxiously and milled about.

"Sumbitch killed the best damn one!" Morning Woman swore and tried to claw her way up to her feet in a fit of anger. Slocum took a new, tighter grip on the woman's waist and wrestled the raging she-tiger back down. She arched her back in a desperate attempt to escape his body lock and fought him like a man to get at the mule killer.

"No! They want us to show ourselves. Stay down!" Slocum pointed to the ground under them. However, she was not to be dissuaded and started up with a grim set to her dark copper lips. Slocum caught her by the upper body and slung her to the ground, pinning her under his weight. Her small fists pounded him on his shoulders as she ranted and raved in her native tongue.

"Dammit be still, he aims to kill us!"

The black diamond eyes of the woman flashed with rage as she glared up at him. "I kill him! The best damn mule is dead!"

"I know. I'll even the score for you, girl. As soon as Pap gets back." Slocum removed his hat and carefully rose up as he tried to locate the shooter's position. The man could have been a half mile away with a telescopic sight on his gun. No signs—Slocum sunk back down. Satisfied the war with Morning Woman was finally over, he twisted around and put his back to the bedrolls and the other things that had spilled out of the pack.

"We wait here. Come dark, I'll go get him if he ain't rode off." Slocum fished out a quirlie from his vest pocket and lighted it. He drew the smoke deep and then exhaled. Another damn score to settle with Hawkins.

Morning Woman said nothing. She folded her arms over

her bust and pouted as she sat on the ground with her hip against Slocum's.

"I'll get the mule killer," Slocum said to try and console her. He pointed at his own chest and made sign language to that effect.

He understood the sign language she made in return. What she intended to happen to the shooter Slocum wasn't at all certain he wanted to participate in. She insisted on making more signs.

"All right, all right." Slocum finally agreed, to silence her. "We'll give him a large enema, too."

The mares in the pen began to act restless as the sun sank down below the mountain peaks. Slocum slipped from behind the mule and went to check on the herd. In the last light of day, he would make a poor target, and he was certain the shooter was to the east, so the sun's glare would be in his eyes. A poor choice of direction for an assassin to make in late afternoon. All hired killers weren't smart; Slocum had learned that through his years of experience on the run, a fact that contributed to his ability to avoid lots of them and survive. Still he considered every threat as very serious.

The hired gun must have become trigger happy to have tried to kill the Indian woman first. Slocum should have been the gunman's target, for Morning Woman was only token opposition. One could only wonder.

Slocum huddled under some bushy pines for cover as he sat on his haunches with the Colt in hand. He tried to take in everything around him as his section of Wyoming slowly sank into the dim light of twilight. The horses were still stomping as if they smelled something upsetting. A grizzly? Slocum hoped not.

He turned to the whisper of her leather soles and the whirl of her buckskin fringe. Morning Woman dropped down to squat beside him.

"Shooter gone?" she asked.

"Yes, I think so."

"Pap comes." She pointed to the east.

"Good," Slocum said as he rose to his feet. She knew the hoofbeat sounds of familiar horses better than he did. Where had the shooter gone? Maybe Pap had passed him on the trail. The two rose and went to meet Pap.

"Got that gun you wanted." Pap said, spitting to the side. Upon seeing the dead mule, he frowned in disbelief. "Who in the hell killed that one?"

"You pass anyone on the way in?" Slocum asked. "I figured you either rode by the mule shooter or he hid from you."

"Few miles back I run across some dumb, four-eyed sumbitch without a hat whipping his horse like Billy Bejesus was after him. He just stopped for a minute. In his early twenties, kinda shook. Told me to watch out for Injuns, that they'd shot at him. That's how he claimed he lost his hat. Come to think of it, he did have a fancy riflebutt sticking out of his saddle boot. Went on toward Cheyenne hitting it hard." Pap spit again.

"Indians attacked him?" Slocum frowned, wondering what the man had meant. "Why, that's crazy as hell. I ain't seen an Indian all day but Morning Woman, and she was with me, though she'd sure've castrated him or worse for shooting that mule. You know his name? Who he works for?"

"No, but I won't forget his face. That dumb sumbitch shot my hard-earned mule and is going to answer for it. I've got half a mind to ride back and skin his ass tonight."

"We ain't got time. I figured Hawkins hired him by telegraph, don't you?"

"Probably so." Pap spit off into the darkness to vent his anger. "Why the hell did he shoot the damn mule?"

"He aimed to kill that squaw of yours and hit the mule instead."

"Damn glad he didn't get her; she cost more than the mule."

"I agree," Slocum said. "You did get the fifty-caliber Sharps?"

"Here it is. Why, she's smooth as a new baby's butt." Pap dismounted and handed the rifle to Slocum. "She's been well cared for, and the barrel rifling ain't even pitted."

Slocum examined the long gun carefully. The wooden stock had been polished with paraffin. The firelight's gleam on the rifle's bluing showed him the rifle's past good care. He broke open the breech and stared down the rifle grooves, clean and unpitted like Pap promised.

"She ought to do," Slocum said, wishing he'd had the long-range rifle earlier to answer the shooter. "Thanks."

"Good used ones like that are scarce as hen's teeth back there," Pap said. "Everyone in Cheyenne has the get-rich-buffalo-hunting-fever."

Slocum half laughed. "I don't know about getting rich, but their asses will sure be a-dragging after a day's shooting and skinning them big devils."

"They damn sure ain't never done it before or they'd know better. And you're damn right about how hard the work is. You and I both know, don't we?"

Slocum nodded. He wondered how he could hire all of Blue Feather's warrior women to help them buffalo hunt. Somehow squaws could do more work in a day than any number of white men and boys when it came to skinning and butchering buffalo.

Pap started at something and instantly went for his pistol.

"You hear something out of place?" Slocum hissed, taking the plate of food the Indian woman handed him.

"Something's out there," Pap said with his head turned to hear better.

Slocum listened to the night wind. He recognized the soft shuffle of the mares, the breeze in the pine boughs, but nothing else. If Pap heard it, there undoubtedly was something out there in the starlit night. Damn, who and what? Slocum pursed his dry lips together and wondered as he listened harder.

Dawn spilled over the mountainside, welcoming the new day. In the distance the mournful whistle of a Union Pacific locomotive rolled across the land. Slocum sat on his haunches with Pap finishing his coffee. They'd taken turns at guarding through the night. Nothing had shown up. The would-be shooter, Pap felt certain, was headed back for Cheyenne and probably more instructions. Still, an edge of something concerned Slocum as he tossed the tin cup in Morning Woman's kettle of boiling water. Nothing he could place his finger on—still his keen senses in the past had afforded him some narrow escapes. Several times too close for comfort.

"Two days and we'll be on the Laramie River?" Pap asked.

Slocum checked the sky. Clear azure blue, no signs of a storm gathering, but still he felt something was about to happen. He hated to ignore his gut instinct.

"Let's push them hard today," Slocum finally said. "I want my back to a friendly wall when we den up again. There's some folks there I know that can't be bought off."

Pap gave him a sharp nod of understanding as he finished tying down the pack on a stout mare they had selected to replace the dead mule. As they completed breaking camp, Morning Woman fussed at both of them about her dead mule and how she aimed to treat the killer when she found him.

Slocum stuck his foot in the stirrup, swung his chap-clad leg over the bay's rump, and wondered where the Shoshone women were at, especially the hard-bellied Blue Feather. They would no doubt rejoin them on the Laramie side of the mountains. He fished a quirlie out of his shirt pocket and lighted it on a cupped match in his hand. He took a deep, satisfying drag and set spurs to the gelding. They had lots of ground to cover before dark.

The sun had long cast the last shadows of day on the valley. Slocum could make out the dark outline of the windmill and the shapes of the haystacks. He turned the spent bay in the driveway and spurred him for a last surge, knowing the herd would follow.

"Friend or foe?" a man asked, armed with a lantern in one hand and a double-barrel greener in the other.

"Slocum, that you, Rip Bell?"

"Yes, sir, Captain. Man, you are a sight for sore eyes. Say, that's a large string of horses coming behind you."

"It sure is. If you'll open the corral, I'll fill you in later."

"Yes, sir." The man rushed to obey. "Hey, Lucia, the man's here!" He shouted over his shoulder.

"That you, Slocum?" a woman asked, coming out on the porch. She busily wrapped herself in a blanket for warmth and cover.

"Nobody else. How's the best cook this side of Dixie?"

Slocum stepped off the bay. Rip had the corral gate open and the mares were filing in as Slocum took Lucia Bell in his arms. Her fiery mouth met his in more than a sisterly kiss. Grateful for the darkness of night to hide her strong show of affection, Slocum savored the moment of contact with her when the blanket fell open and her firm, voluptuous body under the thin nightgown pressed against him, bringing back memories of hot nights long ago.

"You look damn good, Lucia," he said, holding her at arm's length. "Ranching and married life have sure been good for you."

"You don't look bad yourself for a man who can't hang his hat over three days at a time on some love-struck widow's door peg."

"Things going good here, aren't they?" He motioned to the ranch and the rest.

"We're doing just fine." She closed the blanket quickly to cover herself and smiled with a wicked wink for Slocum's sake. He knew by the grin she hadn't forgotten those long ago days either. "Come inside; you look wrung out."

"I am; we been pushing to get here and see you two. I've got some helpers in this horse deal." Slocum tried to protest, but too late. Her arm was securely linked in his, and she firmly steered him toward the house.

"Rip'll bring them in. You know how he gathers strays."

"Wyoming ain't hurt you a bit," Slocum said, admiring her in the lamplight of the house.

"Best thing ever happened to me," she said. Lucia swept the stubborn wave of chestnut hair back from her face.

"You two working together must really be pulling to make this ranch work."

"Damn you, Slocum!" She pointed a threatening finger at him. Then she could not hold it any longer and laughed. "Well, every day ain't a damn sweet bowl of peaches, but I never believed you, never believed when I hauled my butt out of Miss Arnold's parlor house that Rip Bell and I'd ever make it together on a ranch in Wyoming."

"How long has it been now?"

"Five good years and I'm grateful. You hadn't pushed me into this—I just don't know I'd've ever done it. You knew that man out there better than I did," she said and smiled privately at him before the others came inside.

"Lucia," Rip shouted as he burst in the doorway, "this is Pap and Morning Woman."

"Nice to meet you. You all sit down. I'll have some grub ready in a minute," Lucia said, pausing for a brief second to study the Indian girl.

"Kind a young, ain't she?" Lucia asked Slocum as she swept past him.

"That's Pap's woman."

"Oh." She hurried off to stoke up the fire.

After the meal, Rip, Pap, and Slocum went out on the porch to smoke. To Slocum's surprise, Morning Woman had lots of things to say in English to Lucia as they cleaned up the table and the dishes.

"How's ranching going?" Slocum asked.

"Be a damn sight better if we could sell the Indian agencies in this territory our beef. Only way we can sell our stock is to drive it out to Cheyenne and lose all that weight plus have to pay the freight going east as well."

"Who's beef are the agencies buying?"

"They're buying culls from their cronies."

Slocum nodded. "The Indians ain't happy either about what they're getting."

Rip laughed. "Hell, neither would you. They take them poor red devils the old shelly culls you couldn't sell any-place else on God's green earth. Trail-sore old cows and limpers that are so thin you can read a newspaper through them are all they deliver on those contracts."

"I understood those cattle are bought on the bid basis. How do they get the bids?"

"That's done in Cheyenne in this district." Rip shook

his head as if any change there were impossible. "It's all crooked as a barrel of snakes."

"Can you and the other ranchers get up enough beef for these allotments if something is done about the rigged bidding?"

"You bet your life we can."

"What the hell's going on inside that brain of yours, Slocum?" Pap asked.

"We get these mares delivered," Slocum said. "We may have a solution that'll help the Shoshones and the ranchers."

"Be some mighty grateful ranch folks around here if you could get something done about Indian beef contracts. Say, these horses you brought in ain't stolen, are they?"

"Nope. However, they do need a few days' rest and water so Pap and I can deliver them up on the Wind River. If I wanted to hire some thugs up here, who would I go see?"

"What for?" Rip asked.

"Yeah, what do we need some thugs for?" Pap asked as he rose in his chair and spit over the porch railing.

"I figure that Hawkins has already wired ahead and done that. I'd like to nose around tonight see if he has."

"There's a bunch of no-accounts hang out at the Elkhorn Saloon. Pete Donovan would do the hiring."

"That sheriff we got here ain't no better," Lucia said from the doorway.

"Aw hell, honey," Rip said and laughed, "you just don't cotton to how that man looks at a real woman."

"Real woman! Sheriff Elton Suggs is a leering, lying devil."

"Hell, Lucia, if it's you he's leering at, I'd say he was a man of good taste," Slocum teased.

"That's all right, you bunch of smart mouths, mark my words. You better watch him real careful-like. That one is going to be trouble." With a switch of her shapely hip, she left the men alone.

"You headed for civilization?" Pap asked when Slocum rose to his feet.

"Yes, but you better stick close here with Rip. I ain't so sure our arrival here in the Laramie country was a total secret to our enemies."

"We'll handle this part," Pap said. "Keep your eyes peeled."

"I'll do that, thanks. You got a fresh horse in the shed?" Slocum asked Rip.

"A dun. I'll come help you saddle him."

"Thanks. Don't wait up for me, Pap," Slocum said over his shoulder as he and Rip started out for the shed.

"Didn't plan on it."

Slocum had lots of thoughts on his mind. They were still several days from delivering the herd, maybe even a week and a half counting resting them at Bell's place. And then there was the part about Blue Feather and her tribe needing his help. Where was she anyway?

8

The town of Laramie looked put to bed as Slocum rode the dun up the dark main street. A tinny piano's tune carried into the night air, and yellow squares of light from the saloons' doorways shone on the hitchracks and hipshot horses parked in front. Occasionally the loud lilt of a woman's laughter carried out among the sleeping horses.

Slocum stepped off the dun, hitched the reins, and searched the dark streets for anything out of the ordinary. He was in his own element again, nighttime and street and saloon fighting were more his style than long-range gun shooting.

He slipped though the batwing doors into the Elkhorn's smoky interior. Slocum edged carefully to the bar, nodded to the bartender to bring him a draft, and studied the room at his back in the mirror across the bar. Men busy at cards were being pestered by the saloon women, who feared it was growing late and had little to show for their evening's efforts.

Then Slocum noticed the bar girl sitting on the arm of a man's chair. She was busty and the half rounds of her breasts almost exploded out of the low-cut dress. Trying to rub some business up with her hands, she was snake-like, massaging a potential customer's shoulders and chest. Her charm and skill were enough to stir up any red-blooded man observing her. Slocum even felt a little worked up watching her.

But the man that the bar girl pestered was the main reason Slocum found the pair so interesting. In his early twenties, he was tall and wore glasses. A coincidence, but he could have ridden over the mountains from where the mule was shot, and he fit Pap's description of the shooter he'd met on the road.

"Come on upstairs with me, honey," she pleaded.

"I can't!" the four-eyed man under the uncreased new hat protested. "I'll lose my damn job. He won't need me anymore!"

"I don't know who he is, but I need you, darling," she said and stuck out her lip in a pout.

"Elijah Hawkins is who I'm talking about. He'll be mad as hell when he gets here."

"Honey darling, I ain't mad at you and I know you got two bucks. Come on upstairs with me. Why, in a few minutes you'll forget all you know about this Eli Hawkins fella. Whoever he is."

"Dammit, that ain't the problem. I messed up bad. Hawkins's going to be mad as hell at me—"

"Are you turning down my best offer?" she asked defiantly, standing before him with her button-up shoes set apart and her hands on her shapely hips.

"It ain't that!" the man said.

"What is it then? You too damn good these days to go to bed with me?"

"No! That ain't so, Rose."

"Then what is it, Robert Waverly?"

"Not you—Rose. I'm just in deep trouble. Hawkins gets here on the train noon tomorrow. My ass may be dead."

"Oh, the hell with your ass!" Rose stalked away in a

flurry of petticoats and skirt. She started across the room in a fury, headed for the rear staircase. Then she slowed her speed and her eyes narrowed to see if she recognized Slocum at the bar. The anger on her face softened quickly at the sight of this new prospect. A new-business look spread over her pale face as she considered him. Hands on her hips, she began to stroll deliberately toward Slocum so he could view all her assets.

"You sure look lonely, cowboy." Rose stepped beside him as he lighted a quirlie and let the smoke rush out his nose. "My name's Rose."

"Proud to meet you, Rose. Yes, I could be lonely. Who's your boyfriend?" Slocum gave a head toss toward Four Eyes.

"That sumbitch." She gave a contemptuous sneer in the man's direction. "He ain't no boyfriend of mine." She fussed with Slocum's shirt, like she needed to straighten it. "Order me a drink if you want any company. House rules, you know."

"Hell, we wouldn't want to break no house rules, would we?" Slocum grinned big at her. "Barkeep, bring this lady some tea."

"Tea?" She frowned at him.

"Ain't that what they always bring you girls, tea? And I pay for good whiskey?"

"You're a big joker, I can tell." She looked like she wasn't sure how to take Slocum.

"What's his name?"

Rose frowned suspiciously. "Why are you so interested?"

"He looks to me like a man who needs you."

"That mean you don't like my company?" Her hazel eyes glinted with a show of impatience.

"Hold on, Rose." A smile set the corners of Slocum's mouth. "I'll bet you two bucks you can't get that boy to go upstairs with you for free."

"Yeah, let's see your money. Hell, I can take him upstairs for free if you pay me two bucks."

"I'll be damned, I never thought of that," Slocum said, acting as disappointed as he could be.

"Give me your money. You just lost that bet." She stood with one hand on her hip and the other palm turned up waiting for her payment.

"You sure outfoxed me, Rose."

"You didn't look like a sucker either," she said, closing her fingers on the money he gave her.

"Have fun," Slocum said, "and don't tell him what happened. It'll make me look plumb stupid."

She stood on her toes and sweetly kissed Slocum on the mouth to seal the deal. "He'll never know who paid for him. I swear it. Did you think for one minute he could resist me when my ass is for free? You just watch, cowboy." She was about overcome with her cleverness.

"You be sure and give Robert Waverly his full money's worth," Slocum whispered.

"Don't worry, darling. He won't be able to walk out of here in the morning."

"Great," Slocum said, giving her a familiar pat on her solid butt as she turned to leave. She never looked back.

Slocum turned back to his beer and watched her actions in the mirror. She dragged and part herded Waverly across the room to the stairs. He still looked halfhearted about the whole thing, but he was going nevertheless. Why not? Little did the man know Slocum had footed the bill for his night's pleasure. Waverly probably thought it was his charm. Slocum waited till he heard Rose's laughter about something up on the balcony, and then he glanced up in time to see the room door shut behind them. Waverly was in Rose's web.

"Another beer, stranger?" the barkeep asked.

"Nope, got to mosey," Slocum said. He touched his hat brim to salute the man and went outside.

Slocum wasn't familiar with the law or the night watchman system in Laramie, so he just stood and waited with his shoulder against the porch post like a man with lots on his mind. Which one was Waverly's horse? Slocum wanted to jam the long gun or mess up the telescope. Somehow he needed to disable this long-range shooter's rifle so he wouldn't know that Slocum had done anything to do with it until it was too late.

Slocum heard the man's boot heels on the boardwalk long before he ever saw the long, black frock coat and dark hat.

"Evening," the deputy said.

"Evening," Slocum said.

"Guess you're with the bunch coming from Cheyenne?"

"Got in late this evening," Slocum said. He tried to catch his breath as evenly as possible, for he hoped the man would continue with his patter.

"I thought all of you were coming by train."

"I've got a damn good horse."

"Yeah, those damn trains clack you to death anyway, huh?"

Slocum nodded.

"Sheriff be glad to serve that warrant your boss is bringing with him."

"Yeah? How's that?"

"Why, everyone around here knows he's got the hots for Bell's woman. Way I figure it with Bell in the pen from horse rustling, Suggs will have easy pickings on that gal."

"Never know."

"Hell, you ain't been around here before. That damn

Elton Suggs has had such a bad case on the gal ever since she and that husband of hers bought that ranch. I figure Suggs will have her and the ranch before Bell ever sees daylight again."

"Ain't no concern of mine," Slocum said.

"Me either. If Suggs gets her, he won't share her with me or you, will he?"

"I doubt it."

"See you tomorrow at the horse-thief capture," the deputy said and went off in the night. His boot heels grew more distant.

"I'll bet not," Slocum said to himself once the deputy was gone. Now he had to worry about horse stealing warrants for himself, Pap, and Rip Bell. Damn, those outlaws used the law to their own purposes. Slocum spotted what he thought he wanted on the third horse at the rack. He studied the shiny butt plate on the rifle under the stirrup skirt. That was no common long gun. He stepped off the porch and looked around casually as he moved between the animals. The bay grunted when Slocum gave him a push to make room.

A cranky horse on the end of the line gave a pig-like squeal and kicked at the horse next to him. Slocum waited for things to quiet down. As the horses shifted their direction, Slocum drew out the custom rifle.

In a moment he had the chamber unloaded. With the knife from his belt he shaved off a chunk of lead from a .45 bullet out of his gunbelt, using the seat of the saddle for a cutting board. He looked up and down the street. Nothing appeared out of place. Confident, Slocum dropped the lead into the chamber and then forced it forward into the barrel with the bullet he had removed earlier. Satisfied the casing was seated, he eased the action closed.

He slid the rifle back in the scabbard and patted the bay

on the neck friendly-like. "Steady, old boy," Slocum said to himself and glanced up at the windows above. Rose had earned her two dollars well that night. Slocum needed to take the dun and get back to Bell's. They'd have to have those mares gone in the next few hours or they'd share a Laramie jail cell. How in the hell did Hawkins ever figure out to get a warrant for stealing?

Lamont Landers was the only one smart enough in the whole bunch to do that. Slocum untied the dun and checked the cinch. From the corner of his eye, he saw something move in the space by the building. Was someone watching him?

He stood, undecided, wondering if he should mount up or remain there. It might be one of Hawkins's bunch. His palm itched as he slipped the rawhide thong off the Colt's hammer with his thumb. Or was that deputy double-checking?

Then he recognized the swish of her buckskin and saw the tall figure of Blue Feather as she emerged and crossed the porch in a bent-over run. She straightened up once she passed under the hitch and smiled before she kissed him. Her strong lips sought his, and Slocum enjoyed hers for the moment as his arms encircled her.

"We have big troubles," Slocum whispered as he held her powerful body to his and savored the ripeness under the leather dress. "Hawkins has the law on us and we need to move those mares tonight. If we don't, he'll take them and we'll lose the money."

"My warriors can take them through the desert. They will never follow them there. Then you can help me stop the poor cattle that they have been bringing for the tribal allotment. They are very thin."

"Where is your horse?" he asked. They'd have time later to discuss their plans at the Bells'.

"The one in the black coat is watching it." She tossed her head to mean back in the alley.

"He already knows you're here?"

"I saw him examine my horse like he had found gold, then settle in the shadows to wait."

"Take me back there." Slocum hated to leave as good a horse as she usually rode to be sold as compounded property at some sheriff's auction. Besides, he didn't like the notions he'd heard about the current elected official anyway, especially his wanting Lucia so damn bad he'd arrest Rip to get her.

"What about him?" she asked.

"I guess by you doing a little fancy showing off for the deputy's sake, I'll clunk him on the head when he ain't looking at me."

"Sure," she agreed as they led the dun into the alley-way.

So that was set. Blue Feather would act the temptress part, and he'd bust the lawman on the noggin.

"We are sorry about the shooter who killed the mule. One-who-runs put two arrows in his hat and he left after that. We did not know he had such a long gun."

"Thanks, that explains why Waverly is wearing a new, unblocked hat. His old one was holey. Were your women close to the horses all the time?"

"Some of us were."

Slocum reached over and hugged her shoulder. "Good. I knew someone was out there. I just wasn't sure if they were friendly."

He wasn't losing his good senses. That came as a relief. Then she halted him. In the starlight, he could see the proud bald-faced horse raise his head as if he sensed someone familiar coming. He twisted impatiently on the lead and turned, probably smelling her scent in the night.

She gently pushed Slocum aside into the shadows of the building and went on toward the horse. Slocum dropped the dun's reins and then unholstered his Colt. In the shadows, he waited and listened.

"Hold up there, Injun gal," the deputy said, coming out in the starlight and circling her with his gun drawn. "What you doing in Laramie sneaking around this time of night? All the damn stores are closed."

"Want whiskey!" Blue Feather said.

"Yeah, you want whiskey, huh? I may give you some whiskey after you show me what you look like under that dress. My, my, you are some classy lady for a damn blanket-ass Injun."

"You got whiskey?" Blue Feather demanded as if she were drunk.

"Right here, lovely one." The deputy drew a pint bottle out of his vest and held it beyond her grasp. "Hold on there, squaw. You take that dress off first, then I'll let you have the whiskey. Maybe."

Blue Feather looked at him as if she were dumb.

"I ain't getting no knife in my gut trying to have some pleasure with you, gal. Get that dress off so I can see if you got a damn knife on you."

Blue Feather had maneuvered him so his back was to Slocum. She started to raise her dress hem. Then stubbornly she stopped and looked hard at him.

"Give me whiskey first!" Straightening up, she put her hands on her hips in defiance.

"No way! You just undress, big Indian squaw. You got to earn this whiskey." The deputy held the whiskey a little higher and motioned with his gun hand for her to go ahead and take off her clothing.

Slocum wished the deputy would holster his gun. Then he could safely close in and knock him out cold. The law intently watched Blue Feather take the dress off over her head and made no move to holster the six-gun. Slocum heard the man gasp at her beauty.

A smile turned up the corners of Slocum's mouth when the deputy finally holstered the gun and stepped in to take Blue Feather in his free arm. The other arm held the whiskey away from her grasp.

The distance for Slocum to cover was short as the deputy teased her with his whiskey bottle held out in his left hand, and tried to press his body against hers at the same time.

Slocum's gun butt made a solid clunk connecting with the man's skull, and the deputy crumpled to his knees with a deep groan. Slocum decided another swift blow would hold the man down for a while longer. The deputy sprawled facedown. Blue Feather hurriedly dressed.

Slocum untied her horse and led him to her as she shook her braids free of the dress collar and smiled. "He never knew."

Slocum winked at her, then he bent over and picked up the whiskey bottle in the dust. He uncorked it and smelled the contents. Mostly kerosene, Slocum decided as he dumped the contents on the prone deputy.

"Bad stuff. Why, he'll stink so bad when he goes in to report the attack, the head lawman will know he got drunk on the job."

"Good! Where we go?" she asked from the back of her powerful stallion.

"The Bell ranch. We need to get moving. How far away are your women?"

"They will met us at the edge of town."

"Good. Let's ride."

They trotted out of the alley, then let the horses lope easily up the main street. There was a light on in the law office, but no one came out. Slocum breathed easier when they had thundered over the wooden bridge and headed for the Bells' place.

Slocum heard brush breaking along the river, and then there were horses' hooves drumming on the road. Several riders were coming up behind them. He twisted in the saddle with his hand on his gun butt to see the half dozen or more warriors galloping behind them. Blue Feather's war party had joined them. He nodded to her in approval, and they hurried on.

"Everyone up and get ready to ride!" Slocum shouted as they reined up in the Bells' yard. "We've got more trouble than a coon dog has ticks."

"What's up?" Pap asked, pulling on his shirt as he came out of the shed.

"Hawkins got himself a warrant for our arrest and to turn over the mares to him as stolen property."

"How did that sumbitch do that?"

"That ain't the question," Slocum said, dismounting and nodding to the Bells as they came out on the porch. "Pap, you and Morning Woman and the Shoshone women can take the horses to the desert and then up into the Wind River from that direction."

"She gets dry out there this time of year," Pap said, sounding dubious of such a route.

"The women know where there is enough water," Blue Feather said to assure him.

"We heard you," Rip shouted. "What do you need us to do?"

"You two better ride with Blue Feather and me. They intend to charge you with rustling, too."

"That no-good sheriff of ours?" Lucia asked.

Slocum nodded. "You had him pegged. He figured with Rip serving time you'd be his for the taking."

"Had it all planned?" Rip shook his head. "Say, if we leave every stock-fence gate open behind us as we ride out of this valley, they'll never get by all the loose livestock to follow us."

"Good idea. Tell the women what we aim to do about letting out all that stock," Slocum said to Blue Feather.

"Might make my neighbors mad, but they'll understand later," Rip said, dragging out saddles and gear for them to ride.

"Will we be able to come back here?" Lucia asked. She wore a jumper against the night air and pulled on her gloves. Slocum heard deep concern in her question.

"Yes, I promise. You'll be able to come back when this is over."

"Good, 'cause I sure have got attached to this place."

Pap and the Indian women hurried with the pack mule and mare. Cinches were tightened and then the gate came open. The mares that Slocum had so hoped to rest there filed out of the gate to the soft *kii-yiiing* of the squaws on horseback. Things were well under way, so by that afternoon, when Hawkins and the law got there, they'd be in the Red Desert country or close.

Apprehensively, Slocum looked to the east. Still several hours of darkness before dawn to hide their departure.

"What are we going to do?" Lucia asked, walking up close to Slocum as the last of the mares filed out of the corral.

"Go stop a cattle drive."

"Sounds like fun. This tall one goes with us?" Lucia motioned to Blue Feather, who was busy giving One-who-runs lots of directions.

"Yes, why?"

Lucia took her time looking over the tall Shoshone in the lantern light. Then with an approving nod, she turned back to Slocum. "She looks more your style than the other one."

"Glad you approve," Slocum said softly and gathered his reins to remount.

"Oh, hell, I got some rights," Lucia said and leaned over close. "I had you first. If I didn't have such a good man, I'd have you again."

Slocum nodded. He watched Lucia hurry back to the house and wondered how he'd ever clear Rip of the horse theft charges. He would have to do that before it was all over. To him, the papers were just like a pestering sweat bee; he'd swat at it and didn't really care about it because he'd soon ride on. Those two had a great life started in this country. The notion would ride hard on Slocum until he solved the matter, and he knew it.

"You're planning to catch up with us out there?" Pap asked, swinging the pack string around.

"Yes, as soon as we get this herd of cattle split up, we'll be coming."

"Good," the older man said.

"Pap, you and that woman of yours be careful. This looks like the best plan I could figure."

"As long as those squaws know where the water is out there this time of year, we'll be fine."

"They do," Slocum assured the man and watched them ride out after the herd. Damn lot of trouble for about four hundred dollars profit. Beat robbing banks anyway, even if they were under indictment for horse stealing.

"Lucia and I figured we'd need something out there to eat and sleep on. We got some supplies from the house. Beans, bacon, and blankets," Rip said, coming down the stairs with his arms loaded. He searched around to be sure he and Slocum were alone. "Nothing I can say seems to help her. Lucia is damn sure taking this hard."

"I know," Slocum agreed, looking up to see the wet-eyed Lucia coming out the front door. Then she blew out the lamp.

9

"That's what kind of beef they're sending to the Indians?" Rip asked in disbelief as they studied the slow-moving herd. "That's worse than sorry, it's unbelievable."

"Pretty bad, all right," Slocum said, lying beside him on the ridge and viewing the herd's passage in the distance.

"Why, a good half dozen of those sore-footed, skinny critters will just lie down today and never get up again. You've seen them do that coming out of Texas, haven't you?" Rip asked.

"Yes," Slocum said, not fond of the memory. Kate Moffet had coaxed him into driving north all the cattle she'd bought cheap to get rich on in Kansas. A well-endowed redhead, she'd been a whole lot better in the bed than as cattle buyer, for Slocum's money. A whole lot better. In fact her skills on her back in the four-poster bed upstairs over the All Right Saloon were the only reason Slocum even accepted the job in the first place. She got the cattle cheap because they were sore-footed, old, and some even toothless. Some liar claimed he stole them in Mexico and wanted out from the deal to avoid being caught with the goods. Lord, by Slocum's book, the Mexicans probably clapped their hands to see such sorry stock leave their nation, because buzzards would have past the dead ones up, they had so little to eat on their bones.

Slocum knew the instant he saw their long horns they were old. Why, some had racks six feet wide and rumps six inches wide. He remembered sitting in the rig with Kate in hot mesquite country as she talked about this get-rich scheme. He wanted to go hang the whole bunch who sold her the cattle in the first place, or, better yet, find them and make them take the sorry things to Kansas for her. All that redhead could do was gush about how Slocum was going to drive them cheap cattle to sell for high prices to some dumb Yankees in Kansas.

Yankees were lots of things to Slocum, but there were not many dumb cow buyers in their ranks. The stupid ones didn't survive long in the south Kansas cow towns. Someone soon skinned them, and they were busted and out of the business.

Hawkins's herd looked like the same bunch of scrubs. The cattle were so hungry they even snatched bites of sagebrush as they ambled along.

"Them ain't cowboys," Rip said. "I can plainly see some are riding donkeys. Ain't a cowboy in the world hungry enough to ride a jackass after cattle."

Slocum opened the brass telescope he'd brought from his saddlebags. He zeroed in on some of the riders. Some were riding mules, others skinny horses, and a few had wooden-footed draft animals to ride. They were constantly whipping and growling at their mounts and the poky bovines. Slocum smiled as he handed the glass to Rip so he could view them.

"You can clearly see what they are by their clothing. They're railroad bums Hawkins rounded up to work cheap like the cattle they're delivering. Of course I don't know many cowboys would drive such sorry stock anywhere except to the glue factory. They'll be a month getting them to the Shoshone reservation with good luck."

"What you got in mind for bad luck?" Rip asked.

"Give me those glasses," Slocum said. "Some of Hawkins's henchmen must be with the wagon or somewhere around the herd. If we get rid of them, the railroad trash will skedaddle for the tracks under an Indian attack, won't they?"

"Lord yes. Do you see any of his henchmen?" Rip asked.

"I see one of them. Lad from old Ireland by the name of Robbie Muldone is under that one shade tree out there with some dance hall girl. I can see her satin dress all wadded up, and Robbie's bare behind is bobbing like a cork on top of her. Hawkins knew what that boy was doing on the job, he'd kill him."

"See anyone else?"

"Yes, the real trouble is on that rise on the far side. A killer called Black Dog is sitting his horse and taking it all in."

"You figure he's seen us?"

"I don't figure so, but we ain't taking any chances. We've got to eliminate that one before we try anything else. He's the most dangerous one I can see. There's one more, but I don't see him out there. A big hulk of a guy they call Quarter Martin. I haven't seen him up here, so maybe he's over on the Laramie side with Hawkins looking for us."

"That's all there is?"

"I think so. We get rid of Black Dog and Muldone, we'll have this bunch stopped. Won't take much to scare off the rest of them. Damn, I wanted to scatter these cattle in some wild stampedes and have this over in a day. Hell, Rip, that bunch of cattle won't even trot away, much less run."

"Those bums will run, though, without leadership."

"That they will, my friend, that they damn sure will."

"How do you figure to run off this Black Dog?" Rip asked.

"Scare him to death."

"How?"

"I'm thinking on that," Slocum said.

"You figure he'll be damn suspicious?"

"He'll be wary, but I think we can do it."

Rip shook his head in disbelief as they eased back down to the arroyo where their horses were staked. They rode quietly southward to the girls' camp. Mentally, Slocum went over his plan again and again. If they caught enough rattlers, then he could find out how tough Black Dog really was. Black Dog needed to be rendered helpless, then perhaps threatened into leaving Wyoming for good. His breed upbringing probably made him more dangerous than Muldone or even Hawkins, for Slocum's money. That was exactly why Hawkins had sent Black Dog with the Kid. Hawkins knew the Kid would do some dumb things in his absence—Black Dog wouldn't. The breed would be all business.

"You must be thinking real hard on how to handle him," Rip said as they rode along. "Fact of the matter, Slocum, you ain't said a word in the last half hour."

"I'll try to do better," Slocum said.

"Scare him, huh?"

"That's the game plan," Slocum said and sent his horse loping southward.

They arrived in camp. The women were cooking a small antelope rump.

"Hey, guys, we're getting better at this hunting," Lucia bragged. "This dumb antelope came right to our little white flag."

Blue Feather looked up from stoking the fire and exchanged a private grin with Slocum. She meant no ill will toward the auburn-headed woman who was passionately kissing her husband as if he'd been gone a month; it was just a private reflection between her and Slocum.

"You seen any rattlesnakes today?" Slocum asked her as he poured himself some coffee from the pot.

Blue Feather made a face at him. "No. I don't like them."

"Before dark, you and I got to catch us several."

"What for?"

"A breed called Black Dog is going to find them everywhere he looks when he wakes up."

"What if they bite us?" Blue Feather asked, looking dubious about his plan.

"You don't let them do that," Slocum said, looking at her sternly.

She hugged her arms like she was cold. "I hate them."

"You help me find them, I'll handle the snakes."

Rip was laughing at the concerned looks on the women's faces; they found small humor in Slocum's request.

Slocum fashioned some long, forked sticks to pin the rattlers down with. He demonstrated how to hold down the reptiles until he could get there.

"They'll bite you!" Lucia said.

"No, we're going to defang them first thing. Black Dog won't know that, will he?" Slocum winked at her to cheer her up.

"I ain't so sure I will either," Lucia said.

"Scatter out," Slocum said to his hunters, each armed with a long, forked stick. "There's bound to be some on the hillside up there and around those clumps of sagebrush."

Slocum had a hard time suppressing his laughter as he watched the two women walk gingerly around any plant or possible hiding spot for a rattler. He heard Lucia say she wanted to go back home where she shot them with a greener if they showed up at her house.

"There's one here!" Blue Feather shouted. With the far end of her snake-getter she probed in the dead bush for the buzzing serpentine.

"I'm coming," Slocum said and hurried to join her.

The snake was fat and thick. It thrashed in the brittle brush and fought being pinned. The dry rattle of its velvet tail was loud as Slocum carefully bent over to secure a good grip close behind its gaping mouth.

"I got him," he said, feeling the sleek muscular form in his grasp. "You can let go now."

"You sure?"

"Yes, let go." Slocum straightened with the thrashing three-foot viper in his fist. "Rip, take a stick and wedge its mouth open."

Rip took a twig and forced it into the wide-jawed mouth.

"Blue Feather, take my knife and come behind those fangs and cut them off flush with the roof of his mouth."

Slocum felt her unholster his knife, then she moved between him and Rip to perform the dentistry necessary to render the big snake harmless.

"Lucia, get a sack to put him in," Slocum said over his shoulder.

"Coming," she said and started back toward camp to secure one. "There's another rattler in this pile of brush," Lucia said, without stopping her descent. "I can hear him buzzing."

"We'll get him next," Slocum shouted after her as he held out the withering, de-fanged rattler. It would be harmless until it grew new ones. A half dozen of theses critters in the breed's bed and Black Dog might not stop running until he reached old Mexico.

By sundown, they had captured and disarmed five good-size rattlers. Lucia was still shuddering at the notion, but Blue Feather had the process down. Single-handedly, she captured the last two herself and brought them squirming in her outstretched hand to Slocum for the de-fanging ceremony.

"There," Slocum said proudly as the last one was sacked. He tied the cloth sack's opening and set them aside. "I'm ready to eat. What's for supper? Snake?"

"Yuck. Because of you, I'll dream about those slithering devils all night long," Lucia said, shaking her head. She brushed a fallen curl back and gave Slocum a disapproving look.

He just grinned in return.

"How did you ever figure all this snake business out?" Rip asked as he took his plate of antelope stew from Lucia. She grabbed another tin platter and filled it for Slocum.

"A sideshow I saw down around Fort Davis, Texas, a few years ago," Slocum said. "Every night, I watched this snake oil salesman who had this Indian who handled the rattlesnakes. They had those rattlers in show after show. I saw the snakes, or thought I saw them, bite both the salesman and the Indian time and again." Slocum said, accepting his plate with a grateful nod and then seating himself on the ground. "I finally learned they were pulling the snake's teeth to do that. They'll grow new ones after a couple of weeks. So if you keep them, you got to be careful."

"I wish I could see that breed's face when he discovers them."

"You may hear him clear back here," Slocum said, chuckling at the notion. "We need to cool them in the creek before we go back and plant them."

"Oh, you can't do that," Lucia said from where she was seated cross-legged with her food in her lap. "Why mess with them like that?"

"Cooling them slows them down." Slocum said. "The hotter they are, the faster they'll wiggle off or strike. I want them kinda numb so they don't leave before Black Dog does."

"As much nasty work as this has been to capture them, we sure want it to work," Lucia said.

Slocum gave her a smug nod as he forked in the tender meat and wild turnips.

There was no moon. Blue Feather's long, bare legs gleamed in the starlight as she smoothly dismounted and quickly gathered Slocum's bridle to hold his mount. Slocum hurriedly wrapped his boots in the strips of blanket he'd brought to silence his footfalls. The horses tied, Slocum undid the sack of snakes from his saddle horn and they started stealthily for the quiet cow camp.

Blue Feather was dressed for battle, in a sleeveless shirt, a loincloth, and her calf-high boots; she silently crept ahead. Slocum let her lead the way; her sense of detection probably exceeded his own. He carried the snake sack in his left hand, his right one ready to brandish the Colt in the face of any opposition.

The camp fire was dying, and the snores of the men scattered around on the ground carried in the night. No guard, Slocum decided. Who the hell would steal those sorry cattle? Carefully, he and Blue Feather appraised the camp.

Slocum stopped to slip a rattler in the empty dutch oven on the tailgate of the chuck wagon. He smiled and nodded at Blue Feather to go on as he put the iron lid back in place. The lethargic serpent would warm up in the vessel overnight, so by morning he'd be a perfect hissing surprise for the unsuspecting cook.

They found the Kid and his girlfriend sleeping in a pile at the edge of the camp. Slocum eased a slithering reptile into her velvet valise and motioned Blue Feather on.

They found the breed curled in his blankets away from the others. Slocum inserted a snake in each side of the breed's saddlebag pockets. Then he let the last rattler out beside the breed's saddle, resting horn-down on the ground, since Black Dog did not use his saddle for a pillow as most cowboys did. The serpent wiggled in under the pile of saddle blankets to escape the night's coolness.

"Damn! Who's idea was this herding business?" a sleepy voice groaned as someone rose from his covers.

Slocum's heart stopped. Both he and Blue Feather dropped to their haunches not twenty feet from the sleeping breed. They waited as the man in the middle of the sleepers shed his blankets and then half stumbled over several others to get where he was going. A few grumbled protests came from those he stepped over or on. Slocum watched Black Dog for any signs of movement. Nothing. Slocum was ready to draw down on the breed's first move. Slocum turned to listen to the steady stream of the man's pissing. The man finally grunted in completion and came wobbling back through the mass of bodies that Blue Feather and Slocum had negotiated so carefully to position their surprises.

Would any others wake up, too?

The man was soon settled under his covers, and Slocum motioned for Blue Feather to move out. To exit where they were at, they would avoid crossing the camp again, but they would need to circle back to their horses. Still, Slocum wanted no one the wiser to his setup.

At last clear of the sleeping herders, they stopped in a dry wash and Slocum stripped off the blanket mufflers on his boots. When he straightened, Blue Feather moved into his arms and they hotly kissed. He savored her hungry mouth and wished they were already set up to watch the action from some distant rise, so he could enjoy her ripe body before dawn burst on Hawkins's cattle crew.

"We should have put one in the breed's bed," she said, laying her face on Slocum's shoulder as he held her by the waist.

"Too big a risk. He might have woken up, too. Where they are will scare him enough."

"I hope so."

"Come on, we need to meet Rip and Lucia on the ridge before daybreak."

Blue Feather wrinkled her nose as if she wanted them to be alone for a longer time, but she quickly nodded in agreeable submission.

"Today we scatter his herders?" she asked, sounding happier.

"Yes, today we do that." Slocum hugged her shoulder to reassure her as they headed for their mounts.

"One more thing, let's unhobble their stock before we go," Slocum said, seeing their riding stock in the starlight.

She quickly headed for the mules and horses grazing in the starlight. Her whisper settled even the frightened ones who awoke from a deep sleep. Waving their arms to herd them, Slocum and Blue Feather drove the horses northward so Hawkins's bunch would have more problems gathering them.

At last they were reunited with Lucia and Rip on the ridge, the four of them poised, waiting for sunup and hoping for a look at the discovery of the snakes. As he lay on his belly, Slocum wondered how successful Pap and the Shoshone women had been in making their escape into the Red Desert country. He imagined that Hawkins had been beside himself with the horses gone when he arrived. The sheriff, too, probably had choice words for their sudden departure, since he planned to own Lucia before the frame job was over.

Somehow Slocum had to fix all the problems he had brought the Bells. Rip and Lucia deserved the right to ranch on the Laramie. There had to be a way to make that straight again and in turn teach the sheriff back in Laramie a lesson he wouldn't forget.

They turned to view the camp at the first cold-blooded scream. From the distance, someone in complete panic was shouting "Snake." His voice carried the near quarter mile to where Slocum and his bunch were lounging on their blankets waiting for hell to break loose.

"They've found the dutch oven one," Slocum said. The sounds of pistol shots only added to their mirth.

"Someone shot the dutch oven," Rip said, hardly able to hold in his amusement. "Did you hear the ring?"

"If they missed shooting the damn snake, at least they got the dutch oven killed, right?" Slocum said for another round of laughter.

The uproar from the herders was tumultuous even from the distance they were away from it. There was more cussing and screams from the cow camp. Slocum wished it was light enough to see more.

Dawn came with herders racing about on foot trying to recapture their saddle stock. Black Dog must have found the first of his personal serpents, for there was more shooting.

Slocum used the telescope to see in the gray flannel light. He spotted the breed riding his own horse and rounding up the others' stock. Slocum swore under his breath; he'd hoped the snakes would get Black Dog before he could assume any leadership role. Slocum knew that Black Dog was searching for the enemy, for he kept twisting around in the saddle looking in all directions while driving in the horses and mules.

Then the scream of all screams carried across the prairie. Some of the dull cattle were even spooked by the sound

and lumbered to their feet. Slocum tried to center his telescope on the action. There was a stir around a green satin
dress. Obviously the Kid's woman had found her snake, for
someone was shooting the ground up and a state of panic
had ensued again among the herders.

Someone began to hook up the wagon horse. They were
rushing about as Slocum grinned and gave the glass to
Rip.

"I think that snake bit the Kid's girl."

"No fooling?" Rip said, adjusting the brass scope to his
eye. "They sure are getting ready to go somewhere with his
rig. Wait, they're carrying her to the wagon and putting her
in back. Hope she lives to make Cheyenne." Rip laughed
and shook his head in disbelief.

"So do I," Slocum said, lying on his back and studying
the blue sky.

"Here, let me look," Lucia said and took the scope from
Rip. "Say, does that Black Dog guy have a black horse?"

"He sure does. Why?" Slocum asked, rolling over.

"I think he knows we're over here."

"How could he know that?" Rip asked in disbelief.

"Seen the glint off that glass," Slocum said, taking the
telescope from her. He rose on his knees just in time to see
the breed loping his horse toward them. When he focused
the scope on him, Black Dog reached back and undid the
strap on his saddle pouch to grab for something.

A smile turned up the corners of Slocum's mouth as he
watched the breed grope in the pouch then stiffen. You've
found it, Slocum mused, you've damn sure found it!

The snake came out wrapped tightly around Black Dog's
arm. He recoiled sideways. He tried to fling the serpent away,
but he only managed to flail his horse with the snake's tail.
The black horse, in a frenzy over being whipped, and with
the buzzing rattler so close, broke in two. Black Dog went

for his saddle horn, clawing at the snake with his other hand as his mount bucked as if a mountain lion were aboard. Bridle reins streaming, the unimpeded horse tore away in a wild tantrum fueled by fear. Black Dog clung to the saddle horn, screaming at the top of his lungs for the animal to stop.

"He ain't coming over here," Slocum said, satisfied his plan had worked as he closed the scope. The bums were without any leadership, and it was time to take action. "Let's get ready for the Injun attack."

"I'm ready to have some fun," Lucia said, stepping out of her divided skirt.

"A redheaded Injun?" Rip said in disbelief.

"Listen here, Rip Bell, when Blue Feather and I rush out screaming at those bums, they'll probably dirty their pants to escape. This is my part of this Boston Tea Party."

"Tea party?" Blue Feather asked.

"Oh, it's how they fixed scoundrels like this bunch long ago in Boston. They threw the taxed tea overboard. The white men who did it were all dressed like Indians."

"Tea party, huh?" Blue Feather said, sounding unsure.

"Yes, Boston Tea Party," Lucia said. "Put some of that yellow paint on my face."

Slocum smiled to himself as he studied the pair. Lucia's long, snow-white legs were in sharp contrast to the Shoshone woman's dark copper ones as Blue Feather applied the war paint.

"They'll never believe she's Indian," Rip said.

"They may not think we are either," Slocum said. "But I bet they scatter when we come *kii-yiiing* over the hill at them."

Rip gave up and laughed. "You're probably right."

Hatless, with kerchiefs for headbands, they waited in the dry wash. Rip and Slocum sat their horses, ready to charge out at the cluster of men on their mounts who acted unsure what to do next. Lucia, with the yellow and red war paint striped over her face, a bandanna tied around her head with an eagle feather stuck in it, looked almost ferocious to Slocum. With war paint, red hair, and snow-white skin, she looked up to the task, seated on her horse beside Blue Feather, who carried a long pole with feathers on the end. All it lacked was a spear point, Slocum decided. In their haste to escape, the herders would never suspect it wasn't real.

"Shoot over their heads; we just want to scare them," Slocum told his co-warriors. "Any sign they want to shoot back and we'll take them out. But I suspect none of these have any fight left in them. Not a one of them has even had the nerve to go back to camp since the snake ordeal began at daybreak. Let's ride!"

They burst out of the wash screaming like mad raiders. Slocum checked his horse to a lope and indicated for the others to do the same, knowing they would soon overrun the men if they didn't.

The wide eyes and shouts of the dismayed herders told the whole story of no opposition. There was no decision to be made but retreat. Men went to plow reining and spurring their mounts. They immediately headed the horses back for old Cheyenne. The situation brought a confident grin to Rip's face as he rode stirrup to stirrup with Slocum.

"We got them hoss!"

Slocum agreed as they again began howling like banshees and the girls joined in.

The ragged-clothed army was whipping individual burros, mules, and horses in a race for their very own survival. Few looked back; most hunched forward and rode for all they could. The horse riders soon outdistanced the burro- and mule-mounted ones, but they were all leaving.

Slocum reined up and his three fellow "Indians" drew up beside him.

"Shoot, I wanted to scalp one of them anyway," Lucia said.

"Yes, or kill one with my lance," Blue Feather said as she tossed the long stick aside.

"Sorry about that, gals, but we've got more important things to do. We'll swing back and destroy the wagon and any supplies we can't pack off with us," Slocum said. "Then they can't double back and use any of it in case they try to regroup these cattle."

"Then what?" Rip asked.

"Go find Pap and the Shoshone women. We've got horses to deliver." Slocum cast his gaze westward, and he hoped Pap was getting along. He'd feel a damn sight better when he knew how the old man and the Shoshone women were doing.

10

Slocum topped the ridge, reined in his horse, and turned to look back. Rip's horse hopped up the steep portion behind him. Rip also brought on the three pack animals loaded with Hawkins's supplies. They'd managed to find enough animals to load the goods onto. They had three mules, which probably had been part of the chuck wagon teams, but none were in the same class as Morning Woman's lost mule. Lucia and Blue Feather trailed them farther down the slope and kept the pack animals going.

They should be near where Pap, the women, and the horses were headed, since they'd taken a shortcut to meet them. Blue Feather thought Pap and the others would be close to a semi-dry lake called No-Water. Slocum hoped they would be able to join up with them before the day was over.

He scanned the open desert country far to the south. A long line of white-topped wagons struggled westward distorted by the heat waves. They looked like something from a fantasy, with a mirage lake stretched between him and them.

"Which way?" he asked Blue Feather as she and Lucia drew up beside him.

She pointed southward. "A half day's ride yet."

Lucia, beside Slocum, mopped her face on a kerchief.

"Whew, it sure is hot out in this country," she sighed. "I'd sure rather be home on my ranch. It's a dang sight cooler there than it is here."

Slocum indicated that he had heard her comment and booted the bay off the hillside. The others followed him. He still had the trumped-up charges to resolve for the Bells' sake. To finance anything like a lawyer, he really needed the proceeds from the sale of the mares. A lot hinged on the sale of the Texas brood stock.

They reached the No-Water in late afternoon. Blue Feather led them to a small sweet-water spring on the south shores of the wide, dry flats. Among some large boulders that looked like giant hailstones, they made camp.

"No horse herd tracks here," Slocum said as he remounted his horse. "So I'll ride east and check on them."

"Wait," Blue Feather said. "I will go, too."

"You two keep your eyes peeled. We're going to locate Pap. We will be coming back soon," Slocum said.

"Go on," Lucia said, squeezing his leg as she stood beside him. She squinted against the sun to look up at him. "We know you two want to be alone and that's the real reason you're leaving us." Her wicked wink drew a disapproving head shake from Slocum as he backed the bay away.

"Don't you two do anything either," Slocum said as he turned the horse to leave.

"We won't!" Lucia said. "It's too damn hot for that."

An hour's ride south, Slocum stood up in the stirrups and searched the country far to the south and east for any signs. The heat waves distorted his vision, and he sat back down again concerned about Pap's whereabouts.

"The woman is your old love?" Blue Feather asked, riding up beside him.

"Once," Slocum said. The hot wind bathed his face, and he squinted his eyes against the glare.

"She has not forgotten you."

"She has a good man now and likes her way of life."

Blue Feather agreed. "But she still wants to own you."

"Oh, she just talks."

"Talk I hear and I see with my eyes."

"So?"

"She is good woman. I don't blame her, I would own you, too."

"Oh?"

"But I know you are like the eagle. You fly far and do much for others."

"Not that much for others," he said with a shake of his head. "Let's ride." He booted the bay into a trot. Her talking about eagles and supernatural stuff made him feel edgy. Problem was, she knew more than most did about him, the way he lived and where he had been. The Shoshone woman was a fair fortune-teller. Slocum just didn't want to hear when the end would come. She probably knew that to the day and the minute. He liked living his precarious style of life, and he damn sure didn't want to know when it might be over. Let that come as a big surprise.

Where the hell was Pap? He wiped his neck dry with his kerchief and then lifted his felt hat to air off his hair. Too hot out there for a felt hat, and the damn sun was too hot not to wear it.

"There is a water hole in the dry wash over there." Blue Feather pointed southward.

"Good, let's go. I need a cooling off."

They trotted their horses in that direction. When they topped the third rise, Slocum saw the gnarled cottonwoods that lined the long pool of water. These good watering spots on occasion popped up in a normally dry creek bed. They were fed by underground streams that sucked the flow back a mere hundred feet downstream. Red-winged blackbirds crackled in the swaying rushes.

Slocum drew a deep breath and dismounted heavily. Numb from the heat, he loosened the saddle's cinch. A quick check around the desert and he began to undress. On the other side of his horse, he saw Blue Feather removing her clothing. Slocum smiled at her beauty as he laid his holster on top of his shirt. Straightening, he looked around, imagining the water's relief. Quickly he shucked his boots, pants, underwear, and hat into the pile. Taking careful steps on the burning sands, he tiptoed after her bare cinnamon form.

He admired her long, smooth hips, her skin that gleamed in the sunlight. Then he waded after her with a rush into the water that soon came to his waist. As if a bolt of lightning had struck, he saw from the corner of his eyes mounted Indians appearing on the top of the hill beyond the cottonwoods.

He froze for a moment. Slocum's heart hit some long, hard strokes in the moments before he whirled and charged for his gun. His legs bound by the water, he took long strides, intent on reaching his weapons.

"Hey!" a voice shouted from behind him, "ain't you got more to do than take another damn bath?"

Slocum stopped and blinked his eyes. That was Pap's voice. There could be no mistake about that. Slocum turned slowly to watch the Shoshone women come riding pell-mell down the steep, sandy embankment, making their yipping war whoops. They bound off their horses, stripping off bows and clothing in a wild race to see who would be first in the water.

In a flurry of bronze bodies, they charged into the

hole in great splashes and spray. Their noisy chatter and shrill screams shared with Blue Feather, they seemed to ignore Slocum, who sat on the ground considering the turn of events. Pap rode around on his horse to join him.

"Guess you got the mares?" Slocum asked as Pap dismounted.

"Of course. They're coming now," he said as the horses came down the slope in a long file. "We couldn't resist sneaking up on you."

"I couldn't have either. Any sign of Hawkins?"

"Nope, never saw a soul till One-who-runs saw you all coming here, and we planned a surprise."

"A good one." Slocum slapped his bare knees. They had damn sure surprised him.

"You get the cattle drive stopped?"

"I think we fixed that part." Slocum went on to tell about the snake attack.

"One thing you can figure," Pap said ruefully, "we've done made a real enemy out of Hawkins and his crew."

"You know that water looks nearly as good as seeing you. Since those gals don't mind being bare naked, why the hell should I?"

"Damned if I know, sir. I'll just get me a good seat right here and watch."

"Pap, I doubt you'd get the pneumonia getting in."

"I just don't want them squaws all giggling about how big mine is. Might want to marry one of them one day, and I'd want her to be plumb surprised!" Pap slapped both pants legs in his amusement. "I sure would want to surprise her."

Slocum just rose and went into the water. Hell, he didn't care who saw what. The water looked too damn inviting in the heat.

From out of nowhere, two of the women piled on Slocum's shoulders and more tackled him. He went down fighting under a pile of bare breasts, butts, and laughing women. Slocum barely managed to emerge to the surface by fighting aside two strong women. He grapped a quick gasp of air and found he was outnumbered again. In good fun, he flung his bare-skin tormentors both to the right and left until everyone was out of breath and they settled in the water.

Gaining his sea legs, Slocum finally straightened up on his feet and slicked his hair back with his palms. He heard one woman shout in her tongue and point at him. The others giggled.

"What is so funny?" he asked Blue Feather.

"She wants to know are all white men so big?" Blue Feather said, looking a little embarrassed under her dark complexion.

"Most are bigger," Slocum said and tossed his head toward Pap.

"Is he?" Blue Feather asked quietly.

"Check him," Slocum said.

Blue Feather spoke to the women in Shoshone. In a minute, a half dozen of the young women were on their feet and racing for the old man.

Slocum saw that Pap realized too late that they wanted him. He had barely made it to his feet when they tackled him, and despite his shouting to stop, his clothing and boots flew everywhere. In a few minutes, the proud captors brought Pap to the water's edge with his arms pinned to his sides.

Everyone in the pool looked inspectively at him as the old man frowned at his own state of undress and exposure. Then the women in the water nodded at one another over what they saw. Slocum could hardly contain himself. The snow-white hair on Pap's skinny chest drew a sharp contrast to his holders' brown skin.

"I don't need no damn bath!" he protested. Too late they had him in the pool and underwater.

"Maybe he is bigger," Blue Feather said and ducked her head as if fending being hit, seated in the water beside Slocum.

"He may shrink in the water, too." Slocum chuckled at his own joke. Pap was getting dunked good by the playful women. The old man fought hard, but the women were athletes, as Slocum had learned.

"We go north from here across my people's land," Blue Feather said.

"Yes, we'll get the Bells and cross the wagon tracks and head for your homeland. I can help, but what will your people do for meat without that herd?"

"There will be many hungry children crying out in the night from stomach pains. But there was no meat on those cattle to feed them."

"I guess you're right," he agreed as he watched her rise to her feet.

"Enough!" Blue Feather shouted before she broke into Shoshone, ordering her warriors to get out and get ready to ride on.

Slocum smiled at Pap as he went past mumbling about crazy Shoshones. It was time to move north.

They'd crossed the main wagon tracks again. Rip and Lucia rode with them. Blue Feather's horse soldiers bobbed on the backs of their good ponies. Some were armed with bows and arrows, others older firearms, but they looked very proud and capable.

One-who-runs rode in from scouting ahead. She had a gleam in her eye as she booted her horse in close to speak to

Blue Feather. Finished, One-who-runs gave a bloodcurdling cry and shook her single-shot rifle over her head. Then she charged her horse on to tell the others.

"What did she find?" Slocum asked, turning back to Blue Feather as they rode on.

"Three buffalo."

"Ahead?"

"A few hours. There are not many left in this land. They are bulls, but young."

"You want these buffalo for your people to eat?" Slocum asked.

"For food," she said.

"Can you find poles for the mares to pull the travois with?"

"I will send some women now to find them. You will kill them?" she asked.

"Yes," Slocum said, patting the Sharps butt plate in the boots. "I have the big gun."

Blue Feather gave another throaty yodel yip to equal One-who-runs's and turned her horse back to tell the others more of their plans.

"What are we doing?" Lucia asked.

"Going to hunt some buffalo for food for these people."

"Great, I've never done that," Lucia said.

"You won't be that damn cheerful after you get in on all the work," Rip said with a frown.

"When did you kill one?" she asked.

"I've butchered them before, and nothing is as tough to skin, gut, or cut up as a buffalo out here in the middle of this treeless desert."

"Oh," Lucia said as she grew more quiet. "Nothing to hang it from like when we butcher at the ranch."

"Exactly."

"A little raw buffalo liver and she'll be a regular Shoshone," Slocum said.

Lucia made a face. "Ugh! Not me. I'm not eating any raw liver."

Slocum swung his horse close to her. "Don't worry, these women will eat it raw. They almost go crazy at a buffalo killing. I tell you, many a child is conceived during the hunting times. Eating liver will get you going."

"Aw, you two are joshing me. How could anyone get worked up with their hands all bloody and smelling guts?" Lucia made another face.

"You'll see," Slocum said, and rode off to make a stray mare get back in the herd. Lucia had her a time ahead. Slocum rose in the stirrups. The blood of the buffalo did turn Indian women on. Maybe they knew they had many meals with each kill, but it excited them and he knew how much from other hunts.

Every once in a while, one of the Shoshone women, unable to contain herself, would kick her pony out of the crowd and go racing across the prairie with the deep cries of the hunter pouring out of her throat. The horses the women rode began to sense the impending excitement and started dancing on their front feet.

"Eat liver raw, huh?" Lucia asked under her breath as Slocum rejoined them.

"Oh yes, it does great things for the spirit," Slocum said, waiting for a rise from her.

Lucia refused to look at either Slocum or her husband. "Makes me want to vomit."

"You'll see." Slocum even felt the growing anticipation of the hunt. He'd wanted to be in the buffalo-killing business with the Shoshone women, and it looked about to happen. He drew out the Sharps and took aim at a white point on the horizon. The .50-caliber gun in his grasp at a quarter of a mile was hardly even sporting to drop one of the shaggy beasts. Each of the animals would be dropped in its tracks and never look up or know what hit it.

The sun was long in the west when One-who-runs returned from her second trip to check on the animals. As she rode by them, she nodded to indicate to Slocum and Blue Feather yes, the bulls were still there. Cheers and war cries came from the women riding behind the herd.

The hunt was set. The work of butchering would be done during the cooler hours of the night. Slocum mopped the perspiration from his forehead; that would be better anyway.

In the distance, Slocum viewed the bison from his vantage point. The others were back under the hill so they did not spook them. Undisturbed, two of the shaggy bulls lay down chewing their cud, occasionally tossing their heads at the pestering gnats that followed them. The third one was on his knees rubbing and powdering himself with dust to repel the biting insects. The hot wind blowing was the only sound. The horses were far down the draw, and they all held their breath as Slocum chambered a round in the Sharps.

"Take your time. You can do it," Pap said and left him. Slocum wished the man had stayed at his side. The tough old ex-sergeant could probably outshoot him any day, but Pap had left the job to him.

His feet wide apart, Slocum adjusted the rear sight until he was satisfied with the distance. With his sweaty cheek resting on the oily-smelling stock, he took careful aim and squeezed the trigger. The rifle's muzzle flew upward at the blast, and the recoil slammed into Slocum's shoulder, which forced him back half a step. The bitter gunsmoke cloud was swept away by the wind. His ears rang from the blast. There was a wait. He had missed. Then everyone inhaled sharply when the pawing buffalo fell on his side with a thud. He was shot hard in the heart.

Slocum unloaded the casing and chambered another round, with his eyes keeping a check on the other two the whole time. Buffalos were extremely fast once on their feet, especially if they were panicked. If they did run away, there would be little chance of ever catching them on horseback. That would mean the loss of lots of meat. The other two bulls acted undisturbed by their silent compadre's fate, as if nothing had happened. They chewed on their cud and occasionally slung their wooly heads at the flies.

Round number two was chambered and the sights set. The .50-caliber rifle's muzzle blast and recoil came in an ear- and shoulder-smashing impact. Slocum only hoped he did not grow to so dread the reactions of the gun that he missed a shot.

Slocum pointed the rifle down to reload. He aimed again, taking lots of time, and finally fired. His target, the one on the left, opened his mouth and bawled in protest then went silent as he crumpled on the ground. Slocum's sweaty finger nearly dropped the shell, but he finally jammed it in the chamber. The third bull was getting to his feet. Would Slocum have more than a fleeting shot at this one?

He pulled the butt plate in tight to his sensitive shoulder bone, drew down as the standing bull raised his tail in some straining sort of position. Slocum squeezed the trigger, the rifle fired, and the buffalo arched his back to run.

Then the last bull collapsed on his butt and fell on his side to the cheers of the Shoshone women, who quickly turned and raced to their horses, screaming at the top of their lungs. Blue Feather nodded her approval, and Lucia drew in a deep breath.

"Close, but great shooting," Rip said.

"Come on," Pap said, "it's party time from now on."

"Rip Bell!" Lucia said under her breath. "Don't you dare get in any damn orgy with these women. I can tell! I can tell! That old man is going to lay with all of them."

"Hell, he must be seventy, and besides, he's got a woman," Rip said as they hurried downhill to their mounts.

"Why don't you just eat some liver and join them, Lucia," Slocum teased, feeling the weight of the occasion lifted from his shoulders as they took their reins from Morning Woman.

"No, sir, I've done lots of things for you, but I ain't eating no damn raw liver. Never!"

"How will you know what you missed?" Slocum asked as he mounted and then spurred the bay up the incline.

"I'll never miss it!" she shouted after him.

Skinning was the first of many hard jobs. When pulled on, the buffalo's wool shed in handfuls, especially in the summertime. So keeping a firm grip on the hide while slicing away the membrane between meat and skin was strenuous work and required much upper body strength. At the end of the day, Slocum knew, the skinners' hands would be drawn tight by the drying blood and would ache so bad from the straining to grip, that tears would run down these women's faces. Slocum knew the effort skinning required. He'd done his share.

During the process, some of the women sat on the ground; they sharpened and quickly resharpened the crude knives for the skinners. As they labored, they reminded Slocum of ants on a hill, as each group worked around their bull.

Blue Feather came running with the first liver lobe in her hand. With blood streaming to her elbow, the pride in her face was hard to deny. Slocum kicked out of his stirrups, took her hand in both of his, and bit deep into the dark red-brown organ. It was so tough, his teeth could not severe the tissues, so he drew his knife and slashed a piece free before his mouth.

Blue Feather stood there appraising his reaction, then she took a large bite herself. She chewed, but her gaze never left Slocum. Like two people anxious to complete the ceremony, Blue Feather quickly handed the liver aside to Lucia, who took a sharp inhale at the shock of the delivery.

Blue Feather stepped to Slocum. Her coarse hand, caked with dried blood, gripped his arm. "Let us leave them."

"Yes," he said, for he saw the sunset's fire dancing in her brown pupils. Yes, it was time, Slocum knew for certain, to share more than the liver and do what two strong spirits must do for each other: revitalize their very souls.

"How much should I eat?" Lucia asked after them.

"Until you feel the pulling," Blue Feather said to her and herded Slocum away across the dying light on the prairie, to a more private place, alone, where their powerful bodies could mesh.

11

"Guess they could track us all the way," Pap said before spitting to the side.

"Some of those heavy-laden travois poles really churn up the ground," Slocum said, glancing down at the ruts. He looked southward, saw nothing, and hoped they weren't leaving too many signs to follow. "Blue Feather says we'll be in the tribe's main camp by evening."

"Everyone's ready for some rest and relaxation," Pap said.

"What did you call last night?" Slocum asked, twisting in the saddle to see the man's reaction.

"That was a war dance. Billy be damn, son, a man ain't never seen copper-bottom squaws go hog-wild till he's been to a buffalo killing one time. Some guy tells me he never seen it happen, I'd say, 'Mister, you ain't never been to no buffalo killing.' "

"I even saw where Lucia dragged Rip out of there last night," Slocum said.

"Aw, hell, Slocum, that girl never was killing-struck nor liver-poisoned. She was worried some of them other worked-up fantails would get her man." Pap slapped his knees. "Why, they'd damn sure took him, too, as worked up as they were, if she'd ever turned her back."

"You're right. Man ain't been there will never know what he's missed, Pap."

"Be fun to hitch up with a half dozen these better-looking squaws and go up in the Powder River with some bull wagons and kill them wooly boogers the rest of the year."

"Doing that every day would kill you off, old man, if the Sioux didn't."

"Hell, it would beat dying in bed." Pap punctuated his sentence with spit.

"You'll never be that lucky," Slocum said, turning to look ahead.

"There is something wrong," Blue Feather said to Slocum, driving her horse in close.

"What's that?" He squinted to see what she meant.

"One-who-runs is coming back. Chief Two Horses is coming with her."

"Is he the big chief of your tribe?" Slocum asked as they reined their horses aside to go meet them. They let their mounts take an easy, short lope across the prairie to meet the pair.

"Yes, he is the head of all the Shoshone," she said over the wind. "If all was well, I am sure he would wait at his lodge for you to come with the meat as a gift and thank you for helping the Shoshone women."

What was wrong? Been so damn many things gone wrong in the past few weeks, Slocum half expected anything. He wondered how Chief Two Horses would accept him. Indians, he found, were each one different.

"Bad news," Two Horses said as he, Slocum, and Blue Feather sat in council on the ground, the formalities of their introductions and purpose already discussed.

Two Horses began to explain his problem to Slocum. "The Indian agency is blaming my people for the raid on the cattle these men were bringing. Agent says that since the Indian agency must pay for the lost cattle, there will be no beef for Shoshone to eat this winter."

Slocum studied the man's drawn face. Two Horses looked tired and old with the concerns he faced for his people.

"Those cattle were bones and too tough to chew," Slocum said. "Who is the man who tells you this? Where is he?"

Blue Feather put her hand gently on Slocum's forearm. "The agent is the one. His name is McFarland. The one who makes the men come for count every other day."

"Maybe I should go see this McFarland," Slocum said and turned to the chief. "Today we bring meat for the children, Chief Two Horses."

"Good. One-who-runs told everyone in the camp. They are very excited. She says you and your people have also helped our women."

"They've helped me. First thing, I need to deliver this herd of horses to a rancher on the Wind River," Slocum said, "but Pap can do that for me with some of your women going along to help him." A plan began to form in Slocum's brain; he had lots to do. Confront the agent first then seek outside help if that failed. Those cattle were never actually delivered to the agency. The contractor had to deliver them to the reservation to collect. How were they twisting the law?

Two Horses nodded. "The Shoshone nation will help you."

"Good. I will try to straighten this out about the cattle. Blue Feather, you take care of Lucia while we're gone. Rip and I are riding for the agency tonight. McFarland can answer to some white citizens about all this."

"Go in peace, Slo-cum," Two Horses said.

Slocum saluted him then ran and jump-mounted the bay. The powerful horse was weakening on only the short grass and short rests, but he had several long rides left in him.

Slocum found Rip and Lucia riding apart, both with sweat-streaked faces, since no one had cleaned up in days.

"What's the hurry?" Rip asked Slocum as he drew rein in front of them.

"I want Lucia to stay with Blue Feather," Slocum said after explaining about the cattle and his plan to challenge the agent.

She wrinkled her nose. "I can go with you two. I can handle myself."

"Safer," Slocum said flatly. "You can't shoot, move, and run like just two of us can if we do get in trouble."

"You're saying you two'll take more damn chances without me?" Lucia's mouth was set in displeasure as she waited on their answers.

"Honey, he means that we can move quicker," Rip said.

"I know what he said. You two go get that guy. I won't be happy, but I'll wait with her."

"Thanks. Glad you understand," Slocum said, motioning for Rip to move out. There was lots more to do.

"Hey! Both you two be damn careful," Lucia said.

"We will," Slocum promised, and they headed to find Pap.

"You're in charge," Slocum said to the older man as they held their summit. "Rip and I will try and handle the agent. If that don't work, we'll regroup and find a new plan."

"Me and them hard-riding gals can do it. I'll have these broomtails delivered to the man, our money collected, and meet you at the Shoshone camp in five or six days," Pap said.

Slocum drew out the package that Ames had given him. It contained the mares' origin, Texas brand inspection papers, and the Kansas brand inspector's comments. "This proves the ownership and gives the man a good title."

"Couldn't read it if I had to but," Pap spit to the side, "by grab I'll see the man gets it." He shoved the package down in his saddlebag pocket.

"See you in a week then," Slocum said and turned his horse away to join Rip. He noticed the long, drawn-out kiss between Rip and his mate. Lucia would be safer with the Shoshone. Hell only knew what was ahead for the two of them.

The Shoshone agency crowded the cottonwoods and elders along the Wind River. Set in a sweeping valley were large pole pens for cattle distribution. A row of army-style tents sat to the side, and tepees were clustered in a village beyond those, with barking cur dogs and wide-eyed children, who viewed their approach. The large log structure with the U.S. flag on a staff in front was the center of the reservation. Several Indian police lounged around in their blue uniforms.

"So this is Shoshone agency, huh?" Rip asked.

"Must be. Looks awful damn official. You just remember we're ranchers and we want to supply the contract beef."

"If we have to bribe the sumbitch."

"Right."

The pair dismounted under the hard stares of the Indian police loafing on the porch. They hitched their horses and went up the stairs to the front doors. In the building's stale air, their boot heels echoed on the pegged floor.

"Could I help you gentlemen?" a small, spectacled man asked from behind a large wooden desk set in the center of the room.

"We've come to see Agent McFarland," Slocum said.

"And who may I say is calling?"

"Slocum and Bell."

"Very good, I shall see if Agent McFarland is busy and tell him you are here. Was he expecting you?"

Slocum finished looking at the elaborate fireplaces on both sides of the room, the trophy animals on the wall. "No, but we're here on business."

"Very good." The clerk shuffled off to the rear and disappeared behind a large door. In a moment he returned. "Agent McFarland will be right out."

"Bell and Slocum, huh?" The agent's great, booming voice filled the room. A tall, bearded, pompous man stood there at his office doorway like he was king with his arms folded over his huge chest. "What brings you two gentlemen to this corner of hell?"

"Cattle business," Slocum said. "We understand that your contractor failed to deliver the beef as prescribed by the law. That you need several hundred head of stock to live up to the government treaty with the Shoshone."

"I don't know what lying sumbitch told you that! The damn Indians already got their beef for this fall. We had that distribution weeks ago. Guess they've squandered and wasted it and now want more."

"The cattle were never delivered," Slocum said. "If they were paid for, that may constitute fraud, sir."

"Are you accusing me of fraud?" McFarland thundered.

"I'm saying there were no cattle delivered and the Wyoming stockmen want to fill that contract with good cattle."

"Good cattle?" McFarland said. "The gawdamn Indians on this reservation got all the government beef that they'll get this year!"

"Maybe Washington will think different. I understand President Grant is very touchy about the Department of Indian Affairs anyway."

"You know Grant?" the agent asked, sounding more subdued.

"The Wyoming stockmen have contacts in Washington," Slocum said.

"I imagine you do," McFarland said as if he was reconsidering his words, and finally crossed the room.

"In fact, they have plenty of friends in Washington," Slocum said.

"Hmmm, so you two have five hundred head of top quality beef you'd like to deliver to the agency?" McFarland acted like he was testing them.

"The Wyoming cattlemen can deliver that many in a month," Rip said.

"I'll have to wire my superior in D.C. and see if we have extra allotments to pay for them. You know the red tape in Washington."

"I suggest you and that phoney contractor dig up the money. Washington won't buy two allotments, you know that," Slocum said. "Since the first ones weren't delivered and were paid for, when the auditors figure it all out, you may spend some time in the federal pen."

"Listen here!" McFarland's face grew red from his necktie to his forehead. "You two will never live to the edge of the reservation to tell anyone that lie."

Slocum didn't have to turn to know several Indian police armed with single-shot rifles had come inside as if on cue and were lined along the wall to his back.

"You threatening us?" Rip asked.

"I'm telling you to mind your own business!"

"I guess that Ohio reporter was right, we ain't to the bottom of this pisspot deal yet," Slocum said loudly. He thought someone was standing behind McFarland's open door, so when Lamont Landers stepped out into the room, he nodded.

"What reporter was that, Slocum?" Landers asked.

"Guess you'll meet him soon enough. Him and several newsmen are on their way from Cheyenne to ask lots of questions about this agency."

"I know several journalists in my home state. Give me one name," the arrogant young man demanded.

"Hell, can't you see he's bluffing," McFarland said, acting displeased with Lamont's appearance.

"This Rebel scum is a very daring man. He and probably this other outlaw with him are wanted for stealing a herd of mares from a friend of mine, Elijah Hawkins, sir. May I suggest you arrest them and we'll hold them in your jail for the proper authorities to pick up?"

"You're pretty damn sure of yourself," Slocum said.

"Definitely when dealing with scoundrels like you."

"McFarland," Slocum said, "when this man falls, you'll swing with him. And he will fall. Don't you get any grand ideas about arresting us. Your authority is limited to Indians."

"And those whites who sell whiskey to the Indians," Lamont said with a sly smile of confidence across his face. "Lock them up till our friend gets here," he said to the agent.

"All right, you two raise your hands," McFarland ordered. "My police will blow your guts out if you try something."

"McFarland, if they shoot, you and Lamont are getting it, too. Those Indians ain't sharpshooters."

"Hold it!" McFarland said, holding his hands up.

Slocum was swift. In two steps he was beside Landers and, to the suave man's shock, his belly gun was buried in Landers's guts.

"Tell them to back off! Now!" Slocum said through his teeth, the only other noise that of flies buzzing.

"What are you doing?" McFarland demanded.

"Tell those police of yours to put their guns on the floor and be quick," Slocum ordered, holding Lamont by the right arm, his pistol shoved into the man's side.

"You'll never live to get away with this," McFarland said, wanting to take down his hands so bad they nearly trembled.

"Shut up! Get a good horse out front for Lamont to ride," Slocum ordered. "He's going with us and be quick. You send a sorry one, I'll kill him within a hundred yards of this building. Now get to ordering."

"Sergeant Thunder," the agent said. "Get Lamont a horse and saddle it quick! We don't want anyone shot here. You men, be calm. No one wants war here."

"Sir," the clerk said, "a telegram is coming in, should I answer it?"

"No, you gawdamn fool!" McFarland swore.

"Move over there." Slocum roughly shoved the senator's son toward the clacking telegraph machine. He shifted gun hands to use the key with his right hand. Slocum answered, quickly tapping out, *Shoshone Agency, open.*

He waited, wondering if that were enough. A smile almost came over his face when the key replied: *Agent McFarland—Shoshone Agency—Wind River, Wyoming—Slocum and others are coming—They must not get by you—Two U.S. marshals by Grant's orders coming too—On my way—Hawkins.*

"What did it say?" McFarland demanded.

"Your partner Elijah is coming. He is warning you about someone called Slocum coming, huh, clerk?"

"That's what it said," the clerk swallowed, "except for—"

"Tell him what else," Slocum demanded.

The clerk made a wave toward Slocum and Rip. "It said

these two are federal officers sent by President Grant."

"President Grant hired you Rebels to handle U.S. government business, I doubt that," Lamont said.

Slocum drove the gun barrel hard into his gut. "You'll just have to find out, won't you? The telegram said so."

"It sure did," the clerk said.

"Shut your mouth," Lamont said impatiently to the man. "It's all your fault anyway he knows what he knows now."

"Rip, take the key along." Slocum indicated the telegraph. "I don't want any more messages being sent or received until the federal troops get here."

"Troops?" McFarland shouted.

Slocum almost smiled; that would give the crooked agent something to fret over. Rip stepped over, took the key off the table, and jerked the connecting wires in two. He stuffed the machine inside his shirt and, gun in hand, started backing toward the door, after Slocum and their hostage.

"Don't even think of trying anything," Slocum warned as he guided Lamont like a shield through the silent rank of Indian police who stepped back for him.

"That horse for Landers look good enough?" Rip asked over his shoulder.

"He'll do," Slocum said, busy tying Landers's hands before him. "Mount up slow-like and grasp that horn. You make one wrong move and the buzzards pick your bones."

"You two aren't U.S. marshals. If you are, I'll have your damn badges before you can wipe your ass."

"Careful with your mouth," Slocum said, mounting up and catching the reins to Lamont's horse. "You may lose all them teeth. When I want you to talk, then I'll ask. I don't intend to listen to your palavering all day as long as I have to put up with you. Is that clear?"

"Yeah."

Slocum turned to the front, "Mount up, Rip; they ain't

coming out shooting with pretty boy amongst us. Ride close to him. Let's go!"

With Rip beating on Lamont's horse with a lariat to make him move, they left the agency at a hard run.

"What's the story on the marshals?" Rip shouted as they topped the ridge. Slocum reined up. The Indian police would soon be mounted and on their trail.

"Best hope that we have. Two lawmen are being sent by the President to investigate McFarland and all this crooked business. The clerk got the message wrong thinking the two on the way were us."

"I knew you two weren't federal marshal—" Lamont had no time to defend himself. Slocum's backhand to his mouth split his lip on his teeth. The blow forced Lamont to draw his bound hands to his hurt mouth. He spit blood and his eyes narrowed in hate.

"When I said shut up, I meant it! Let's ride," Slocum said. He checked the sky; in a few hours it would be dark. The cover of night would help; they'd still need lots of luck ever to be able to outrun McFarland's Indian police.

As bad as Slocum hated to do it, he headed for the main camp of the Shoshones. His going there might cause the Indians some mistreatment by McFarland, but he didn't know the terrain well enough to go elsewhere.

The distant mountain range swallowed the sun as they paused to rest their horses. His bladder empty, Rip walked over to join Slocum. Their mounts were snorting, tired and sweaty; from time to time, they stomped at the obvious muscle cramps in their legs.

"So what about Hawkins?" Rip asked under his breath, satisfied that sullen Lamont couldn't hear them. The senator's son sat on his butt a few yards away where Slocum had placed him after retying his hands together.

"He must have been in Cheyenne when he telegraphed that. Says he's coming, too. I didn't notice the sending office."

"This whole thing is going to blow up, ain't it?"

"Yes, I think so. I hope for the best for the Shoshones and jail for that scum and the other thieves." Slocum indicated Lamont.

"You reckon you'll get that many cattle sold to the agency like you were talking to McFarland about?"

"That's just part of the Indian Bureau's business. If we cut out the crooked contractors, there can be lots of good business for the territorial cattlemen."

"Guess we better ride."

"Yes, load up." Slocum jerked his silent prisoner to his feet then shoved him toward his horse. "Those Indian police will have fresh horses."

"My butt could sure use a rest," Rip said, swinging his leg over his horse rump to remount.

"You've been spending too much time in that featherbed and not out riding," Slocum teased. Lamont mounted, and Slocum handed the reins to Rip.

"Can't blame a man for that," Rip said. "Someday I'll repay you for her and that setup. Kind of a dream come true for the both of us."

"I know it is. No problem," Slocum said with a sigh, "I just get a little jealous of you at times. Thinking about you snuggled up to that fine body of Lucia's when I'm camped on some cold, lonely ridge with coyotes howling louder than the damn wind and only my nightmares to sleep with."

"I know how damn poor that is," Rip said solemnly. "I been there, too."

Slocum made his horse move out. He still had to straighten out the Laramie sheriff for their sake—Lucia and Rip's.

• • •

They'd ridden several hours, and Slocum hoped his instincts were leading him in the right direction. The night sky was full of star holes, and their ghostly glow silver-lighted the low sagebrush land around them. Slocum twisted in the saddle but observed no sign of pursuit. They'd come; their prisoner was too valuable for McFarland not to recover him. As they trotted their horses, Slocum stood up in the stirrups and flexed the tight muscles in his back. He couldn't recall sleeping very long in the past week. A good night of sleep might even revive his brain.

"Riders coming from the west." Rip pointed to the faint shadows on the horizon. "Are they on our side?"

Slocum reached to shift the Colt into place. "I damn sure hope so." He tried to see in the half-light but couldn't. Several riders were coming.

12

"Hold up," Slocum said over his shoulder to Rip. None of the riders approaching them were wearing hats. That meant they were probably Indians and they could be on the warpath, for Indians usually only wore white men's headgear.

Slocum drew his Colt. "One word out of you and you're buzzard bait," he growled at Lamont seated on the horse beside him. "Rip, they may be friendly, they may not."

"I'm ready for war," Rip said with his revolver in his hand, drawing his horse up beyond Lamont.

"Slo-cum?" a familiar voice called out.

"Come on, Rip, it's Blue Feather," Slocum said as a wave of relief swept through his taut shoulders.

"We're coming!" he shouted.

Blue Feather and a half dozen of her women warriors gathered around. Slocum quickly explained the prisoner and the fact that Indian police were on their trail.

"We can handle the police. Switch horses with us. They will track my women to the desert and then they will lose them."

"I don't want any of the women hurt," Slocum said, concerned the agency law might turn brutal if they ever caught the women who had tricked them.

"No worry, we will sweep the ground like you tried to do to hide the tracks," Blue Feather said, then she spoke to her warriors in Shoshone about the plan.

Slocum hauled his prisoner off his horse.

"What're them Injuns going to do to me?" Lamont asked under his breath.

"Oh, probably make a gelding out of you," Slocum said, undoing the girth on Lamont's saddle. "They keep white boys around after they cut them to pick berries and to whip when they get mad."

"Shoot me, Slocum!"

"Why, Lamont, you actually want me to shoot you here and now and deprive those squaws of hearing you scream and plead when they use their sharp knives on you. My heavens, boy, I may stay around for that myself."

"You can't let them do that!" Lamont was searching around in desperation. "Why, it ain't Christian!" he cried.

"Was feeding these poor Indians that sorry beef you and Hawkins been sending them Christian?" Slocum winked at Blue Feather, who had overheard their conversation. "Maybe I should tell them you were the one behind that. Then they'd stake you on an anthill and pour honey on your face. Me, I like the gelding business better. You'd last longer, to remember all the damn dirty tricks you did to these people."

"I promise never to do it again! Oh God, help me! Please, Slocum!"

"I don't give a big goddamn what they do to you, boy!"

In an instant Blue Feather swiftly stepped in, jerked Lamont's belt open, and stripped his galluses off his shoulders. Lamont's pants fell below his knees before the suspenders caught on his arms, which he held out with his hands tied in front.

Lamont's pitiful scream carried across the prairie for

miles. He dropped to his knees and began to beg and plead.

Slocum exchanged a private grin with Blue Feather before he roughly jerked the moaning senator's son to his feet. "I ain't letting them do it here unless you give me cause. But you know now you ain't in Cincinnati, where they protect scum like you. You're in Shoshone country, and they don't like wormy flour and half-dead beef either. They'd like to punish the sumbitches in charge. You understand, Lamont?"

"Oh yes, God's yes. Let me go, Slocum. I promise you I'll get it all done right."

"I'd rather have a bucket of horse piss than your promise. No, I ain't letting you go, but if you try something," Slocum roughly jerked the man's galluses up so the harsh action caused Lamont to bow forward and give a pained grunt, "I'll let them have you, Lamont. Do you understand?"

"I-I won't do nothing but what you say. I promise."

"Get on this horse," Slocum said, having finished saddling the Indian horse for him to ride. Slocum stepped back. The fury still inside him raged like a forest fire. *I promise you!* The senator's son's words weren't worth nothing once Lamont got away. Slocum took the reins to his new horse from one of the women who'd changed his rig over for him. With a nod he thanked her.

"How's Lucia doing anyway?" Rip asked, riding up on his new horse.

"Fine," Blue Feather said. "She's busy helping my older sister with her new baby."

"Lucia is helping with a baby?" Rip asked.

"Yes, why?" Blue Feather asked.

"Lucia don't even like babies."

Blue Feather reached out with her palm and gave Rip a

flat blow on the chest. "Soon she will have one of her own to take care of."

"What! You hear that, Slocum?" Rip called out.

"Yes, I did," Slocum said, readjusting his girth.

In an obvious daze, Rip dismounted, jerked off his hat, and combed his fingers through his hair. "Well, gawdamn, can you believe that, Slocum?"

"Yes, I can," Slocum said, hardly able to contain the humor he saw in the man's reaction. "It happens all the time when folks climb in those featherbeds together."

"But we been married five years."

"Hell, son, you finally did it right is all." Slocum laughed as he swung up. "Blue Feather, we need to head off Hawkins. He's probably headed for the agency."

She made a smooth swing and was aboard her mount. Next she gave directions to the three riders headed south on the shod horses to trick the police. They nodded that they understood and set off, one even leading another squaw on a horse so the tracks would look natural.

The other women rushed about sweeping the ground with sage boughs to cover part of the tracks so the police would have their work cut out for them to separate the shod horses from the pony prints.

The task of hiding tracks completed, they mounted their ponies and Blue Feather took them northward. Lamont had slumped in the saddle, resolved to his fate at the hands of his captors.

Slocum studied the Big Dipper and the North Star hanging high above them in the panorama of star-blanketed galaxies that never ended. He wondered if Rip would ever recover from the shocking news about Lucia's condition. Poor man was definitely in a state. Slocum chuckled to himself—Lucia might be, too, for that matter.

Midday, by circling wide, they arrived at a point on

the Wind River south of the agency, among the towering, twisted cottonwood trunks and low willows. Blue Feather posted lookouts on the road, both upstream and down.

They ate dry jerky in silence. Slocum sat cross-legged on the ground in the shade, listening to the rustle of the cotton-wood leaves and bird cries. A red-winged blackbird scolded him from the windswept willows. With a longing to be free of the sweat and horse smell, and the accumulated grit and itching on his body, Slocum contemplated taking a bath in the stream that rushed over the large rocks before him.

Blue Feather dropped to her haunches beside him. She indicated the nearby solemn Lamont. "The guards will watch him."

"We need a bath, don't we?" Slocum said with a smile for her.

"Yes," she said softly and rose to her feet.

Slocum noticed that Rip was asleep with his back to a tree and his rifle sprawled across his lap. *You can rest there, father-to-be, the women will guard things*, Slocum said to himself as he set out stiffly to follow the swirl of Blue Feather's buckskin fringe and the fine hips that made the hem swish around her shapely calves. He wasn't half as tired as he had thought.

Slocum awoke in the darkness. He listened to the night sounds. A horse snorted close by. He noticed as he raised himself on his elbows that Blue Feather was gone from the blanket they had shared in the afternoon. The cool night air washed over his bare skin as he sat up. A shiver of cold forced his shoulder blades together and made his upper body shake for a second. How long had he been asleep? She should have awakened him. Over the river's rush, he heard her speaking softly to someone in her own language. In his sleep-befuddled state, he began to dress. The recollection of passion's fire consuming her, their bodies meshed together, was a nice memory, their afternoon of bathing and lovemaking still a brilliant star in his lethargic mind.

"What's happening?" he asked when she returned. Seated on his butt, he struggled to pull on his boots.

"I send a woman to the agency at dark. She just returned. She says Mc-Far-land has two men in his jail who say they are U.S. marshals. Could this be?"

Slocum readied his other boot to pull on. "Yes, it could be. There were some lawmen coming. They are the great white chief's men." Slocum swallowed and then shook his head at the idea that the agent had gone so far as to jail them. "Obviously, the man figures on running off if he jailed them. U.S. marshals ain't to be toyed with."

"You want them out of jail?" she asked.

"I want to talk with them first. If I can strike a deal, then we'll see."

"Deal?" she asked with a frown.

"They may want to put me in that jail."

She dropped to her knees and hugged him hard. "I would get you out."

"I appreciate that. But *staying* out of jail, that is my problem."

"They are bringing our horses," she said confidently and rose to her feet.

They are bringing our horses. Slocum swept his hair back and set the hat on his head. She certainly knew what he thought and planned most of the time. Damn, what a witch. Stretching over his head drew a few sharp pains, and he grimaced and stood up. A large yawn. He reached for the sky, wondering how Pap was doing on the horse delivery. Fine, more than likely. If Morning Woman weren't so jealous of all the female help around him, the old man would live several more winters.

Slocum's thoughts turned to the two marshals. What would they think and how would they react to his offer? If they didn't act decent, he'd leave them in McFarland's jail until the whole thing was settled.

"Watch Lamont while we're gone," he said to Rip when the man came to join them at the camp fire. "We're going to the agency to talk with the marshals that McFarland's got in his hoosegow."

"Man, he's taking lots of chances jailing lawmen," Rip said. "Say, Slocum, do you reckon Lucia is all right out there with them Indians?"

"She's fine. You quit worrying. Soon as we get all this settled, we'll go out and get her. Then you two can go home."

"I'm ready. Lamont won't go anywhere while you're gone. I'll keep an eye on him. I guess I just went to sleep this afternoon."

"It was all right. You needed the rest. Besides the squaws all had him under their eye."

"Yeah, he wouldn't want no squaw chasing him," Rip said, amused. "That pants dropping business damn sure shut him up, though."

"It did. See you in a few hours." Slocum mounted up.

"Lots of luck."

"We'll need it." Slocum mounted and rode after Blue Feather and the other Shoshone woman.

"How'll we get them out of jail?" Slocum asked as he rode between them.

"Bad whiskey," Blue Feather said and held up a gallon.

"Bad whiskey, how does that work?" Slocum asked.

"We get the guards drunk, then you can talk to the marshals. They get plenty drunk fast with this."

"You be careful, I don't want either of you hurt."

Blue Feather gave him a playful shove as they rode. "We are warriors, not silly girls."

"I still want you to be careful."

"Yellow-deer and I will be."

At the mention of her name, Slocum tipped his hat to the woman on the horse beside him. She giggled in return. Slocum understood Indian women, they giggled a lot, many times at just being pleased about something.

At the agency, they hitched their horses in a grove of trees across the parade grounds and slipped along inside the corral fences to get closer. The adobe jail had a flat roof. In the starlight, Slocum could see the iron bars on the window and the two men seated on chairs at the door. Both wore police hats and had rifles across their laps.

Blue Feather sent Yellow-deer to them with the whiskey. The woman slipped along the corral fence to a gap in the rails. Once through the fencing, she began singing a stomp dance chant in a drunken tone as she danced her way out on the parade grounds. Slocum grinned as he watched her make an erratic circular path toward the jailers. Occasionally she stopped and took a drink from the gallon.

Each time she stopped, Yellow-deer raised the jug to drink then made a great sigh, replaced the cork, and stood straddle-legged for a while, as if the whiskey had nearly burned her up. Slowly she began her chanting again and shuffled her moccasins in stomp fashion.

"Whiskey!" she shouted to them. Both guards put down their guns and joined her. Each one in turn raised the gallon and took great drinks. She got the bottle back and recorked it, then she went shuffling around in the dust. The guards joined her line, nearly colliding when she stopped to turn and offer them another snort. They quickly obliged her.

Soon the two Indian police were into the dancing business. They were raising their knees higher, and their singing grew louder. The one behind Yellow-deer had other ideas as well. Several times she had to sweep his handy palms off her butt with the whiskey jug. Once more she stopped suddenly, and one of the guards lost his balance. He fell down laughing; the other one tried to pull him up and was pulled down, too.

"Now they are very drunk," Blue Feather said.

"Yes," Slocum said. They crept out of the pen and slipped in close to the jail.

Slocum stepped out and pointed his revolver at the guards. They looked in disbelief, first at him, then at the sober Yellow-deer, who ordered them on their feet in Shoshone.

The two were very drunk and had problems rising to their feet, but they obeyed. Blue Feather took their keys and unlocked the front door. Slocum herded the two drunks into an empty cell and locked the door.

"Who's there?" a voice in the dark hissed.

"Friends," Slocum said.

"Who the hell are you?"

"That's what we've got to talk about," Slocum said.

"Get us out of here, man. We're U.S. deputy marshals that McFarland locked us up. You can't—"

"I haven't got time to talk all night!" Slocum cut the man's words off sharply. "My name is Smith and I need a promise out of the two of you. If I help you out of this jail and we round up all the culprits in this crooked Indian agency, then I want to ride out of here a free man."

There was a silence in the dark jail.

"You asking for a pardon for helping us in this deal?"

"No. I don't have a thing to do with this mess except I'm here helping her people. All I'm asking for is for you to let me ride out of the country when this over."

"Kind of unusual. What charges are against you?"

"That ain't the point of discussion here. You have two minutes to decide," Slocum said and started for the doorway.

"Wait!"

"We got a deal?" Slocum asked, pausing in the doorway.

"Yes, you can ride, but we can't say what will happen after that."

"I don't want a hassle from you two when I ride out of here after you have all this Indian ring rounded up. Am I clear?"

"Clear enough, get us out of here. What's your real name?"

"I told you, John Smith."

"I'm Deputy U.S. Marshal Chester Young. This is Deputy Edgar Milton. For the moment we're glad you're on our side. Who's she?"

"Blue Feather. She's with the tribe."

"Nice to meet you, ma'am," both lawmen said.

Slocum wasn't certain they would keep their word when the conclusion came. However, these men could clear Rip's name. Rip had no warrants against him except the Wyoming one that Hawkins had hassled up over the mares. Maybe they'd keep their word, maybe they wouldn't—Slocum planned to cross that bridge when the time came.

"Remember this," Slocum said to the pair. "You back out on your promise, we'll not end this with all of us standing."

"We understand."

"Turn them loose," he said to Blue Feather and went outside to consider his decision.

"Smith," the blond-haired lawman called Young said as he came out on the porch. "I think we should arrest the agent first."

Slocum was considering the agency's dark, sprawling log building. Where did McFarland sleep? It would help to know the location of his bed inside the building, for surprise purposes.

"Good idea," Slocum agreed, "but he has this key operator that looks like he'd piss in his pants if you shouted boo at him. Let's keep him away from McFarland if you want all the information on how the crooked big man ran the agency."

"His name is Bailey. That's a good idea. But we need some firearms," the older man, Milton said.

"One of you take that guard's rifle. Blue Feather, give them your pistol," Slocum said. "We'll surely find some more guns in the agency."

"I'm sure we will, Mr. Smith. We're ready," Young said, armed with the long gun.

"One of you go with her around back and cover that way out. She can see in the night like an owl, just don't let her get hurt," Slocum said.

Blue Feather and Milton headed for the agency back door. All Slocum could do was hope the lawman had the grit to hold anyone off that tried to escape the back way.

He and Young waited to give them time to take their position, then they rushed the front steps. The door was locked. Slocum whipped out his knife and inserted the blade in the crack between the casing and the door's edge so he could lift the bar. He strained to dislodge it, then the board gave. It fell inside with a crash.

"Too loud," Slocum said with quick regrets, shouldering the door open and rushing in. Inside, he sprawled across the floor on his belly, the Colt ready in his right hand. No shots; he waved in Young. On his feet again, Slocum reached the desk for a place to hide behind should the shooting start.

"Wh-who's out there?" a trembling voice asked, and a lamp came on in a room off the main one.

"Bailey," Young hissed.

"You get him," Slocum said, wondering where the big man slept.

Slocum had only the time to hit the floor when the metallic sound of a hammer being cocked told him hell was about to break loose. The room became ablaze with bullets and gunsmoke. The reports were so loud they hurt Slocum's ears as he tried to take aim at the shooter's form.

The rifle gun blast from the other side of the room made John flinch. Had the lawman hit the agent? Slocum coughed on the thick gunsmoke as he rose to his knees. His eyes streamed from the searing black powder, so thick he could cut it with his knife. Where was everyone?

13

"I'm shot!" McFarland shouted. "Hold . . . your fire."

"Keep your gun on him, Smith," Young ordered. "I'll get a light."

"Damn you, Young, how the hell did you get out of jail?" the agent grunted from somewhere on the floor near the far wall.

"Hold your hands up!" Slocum ordered, more worried at the moment about being tricked than anything else.

"I know your voice. You're the one took the telegraph key," McFarland said as if he could hardly believe it.

"You're wondering why those Indian police didn't get me? They're off in the desert looking for their asses."

"Damn!" McFarland grunted, sounding discomforted.

Young held the lamp high enough to cast the yellow light across the room. Gun in hand, Slocum rose and joined him. The agent lay slumped against the wall. Where he'd been shot was high on the chest and right of the vital organs. It had begun to bleed.

"You ain't half as ferocious without your police, McFarland," Young said as they stood over the man. The agent's gunshot wound didn't look too serious to Slocum; the man would live. "Get up," the lawman ordered.

"What about my shoulder?" McFarland gave his wound a pained look.

"You should have thought of that before you shot at us."

"You broke in . . . here." McFarland strained as Slocum jerked him to his feet. "I thought you was renegades."

"What we want to know is where is Hawkins?" Slocum demanded.

"Who's that?" Young asked.

"The main ringleader of all the skulduggery in the Indian supply business. Don't give me that I don't know business; you and Hawkins are thick as brothers."

"Does he work for L and L Company, this Hawkins?" the deputy asked.

"Landers and Landers?" Slocum shook his head; maybe it was only a coincidence the names and initials were the same. "I'll tell you some more about these crooks later. Let's take him to our camp," Slocum said. "We have some guards there, and let's see if we can still capture Hawkins before he gets wind something is wrong."

"Put me down!" the clerk shouted as Marshal Milton hauled him by the collar through the rear door.

"He was running out the back door like a bunny." Milton laughed as he shoved the man toward the desk.

Blue Feather came in and scooped up the agent's pistol to trade with Milton for her own. She exchanged a nod with Slocum over the agent seated on the edge of the desk holding his bloody shoulder.

"Where is Hawkins?" Slocum demanded of the clerk.

"I-I don't know!"

Slocum jerked the man up by a fistful of his nightshirt. "You better go to thinking and knowing where he is or I'll feed you in bite-size chunks to the Shoshones."

Bailey looked around for any sign of a threat larger or

worse than Slocum before he said, "He's coming with his whole gang. They'll get you guys."

"Hawkins will be wearing lead for his buttons before then," Slocum said. "Let's go to camp. We've got food and coffee there."

"We could use some, thanks," Young said.

A horse was rounded up for everyone to ride. In a short while they were headed down the river road for the camp, with McFarland moaning and grunting in the saddle, and Bailey squeezing the saddle horn to death and shaking in fear. Slocum rode behind with Blue Feather and Yellow-deer.

He wondered how close Hawkins was to the agency. Blue Feather's scouts would know. There might be a good chance to surprise the outlaw when he was in his own camp, unless he was already on the road, headed north to join McFarland.

Young reined up and waited for Slocum to ride beside him.

"How are we doing this?"

"Her scouts will bring word soon enough where the other gang members are at."

"Did you hear that, Milton?"

"Yes," his partner said over his shoulder.

"How did you get hooked up with these Indian women?" Young asked Slocum, casting a glance at the two of them.

"Long story, I'll tell you sometime, but don't think for one moment they won't fight. Oh, one more thing, we have a senator's son as a hostage up here."

"A U.S. senator's son!" Young's voice almost squeaked.

"Ease off. He's in this crooked dealing up to his neck," Slocum said impatiently.

"Who is it?"

"Lamont Landers."

The silence settled. McFarland coughed and then chuckled to himself at the situation. Slocum wanted to hit him over the head.

"Hold up your horse," Young said to Slocum, "and let them go on."

When the others were several yards away, the lawman began under his breath, "Do you know who Senator Landers is?"

"I don't give a damn. I think this boy and his father are the L and L Company. The one cheating these Indians and lots more. He'll knows how many more are in on it."

"But he's the most powerful man in the Congress of the United States."

"A crook's a crook, in office or out."

"Can you prove any of this?"

"Lander's son will talk," Slocum said, about to unfuse at the lawman's attempted restrictions on clearing the matter up.

"Then we'll hear it," Young said, somewhat settled.

"I thought President Grant sent you out here to stop all the crooks stealing from the Indians," Slocum said as he reached out and caught the lawman's arm to make him stay there and settle the matter.

"He did, but damn, man, not to upset no applecart like that. He wanted some locals rounded up and a few agents made examples of to satisfy the newspapers who are up in arms since Custer's speech before the congressional board."

"Landers is in this neck-deep." Slocum waited for the man's reply.

"Milton and I may have to wait for orders."

"I for sure want Hawkins and his renegades out of this game," Slocum said. "Don't get me wrong; I want the big boys, too. But those Easterners could never pull it off without a hardcase like Hawkins to ramrod it out here."

"I agree, but I sure don't like the fact you have the senator's son in your custody."

"I asked you for one thing when I let you out," Slocum reiterated, to hear the man's answer. "When this is all over and you have your arrests, may I ride out?"

"You've got our word."

"Good. Let's catch up with the others. Another thing, a man helping me has a phoney warrant over his head about some stolen horses this Hawkins wanted for himself. The horses are now on a ranch up on the Wind River. They were brand inspected in Texas, and Hawkins never had the bills of sale for them."

"What's this guy's name?"

"Rip Bell. You'll meet him. He's in camp ahead."

"Easy enough, we get Hawkins arrested, we'll make them take the warrant back on this, uh, Bell guy."

"Sounds good," Slocum agreed, "thanks." He felt some relief over that matter. Where was Pap all this time? The old man could take care of himself but Slocum wished he were there to help capture Hawkins.

"I just wish there was a way—" Young shook his head. "Oh, hell, never mind."

Slocum knew without the man saying it that he didn't like the fact Slocum was holding Lamont Landers as a prisoner.

What if? His notion might just work. Slocum rode his horse up beside Young. "Say, what if we won't bring those two into camp to start with. The squaws can guard them, say, a ways away. You two can hide close by, and I'll get the truth out of Landers so you can hear his side of this deal."

"Yes, I'd like to do that. I'll tell Milton your plan." Both men booted their horses to catch up with the others ahead on the dark road.

"Get your ass up!" Slocum shouted and jerked Lamont to his feet. He'd briefly explained his deal with the lawmen and his plans for the senator's son. "Now, start talking! Who owns L and L?"

"My dad—and uncle."

"How many other tribes do you cheat with sorry provisions like you do the Shoshones?"

"Several," Lamont said, nearly chocking on his swallow.

"How many?"

"I'm not sure; there are lots of them."

"How many other tribes do you sell whiskey to?"

"Not many. Other guys sell them whiskey, so we can't get in."

"Why not?"

"We can't find men to do it for us."

"Men like Hawkins."

"Yeah."

"You ever been hungry and cold at the same time, Lamont?"

"I guess not."

"You will be. They say that Detroit Federal Prison is colder than polar bear country. Guess your rich friends, close by, though, could come by and see you there."

"My dad won't let—"

"Think again, boy! Your dad's going to be in there shivering his ass off with you."

"Never—I mean, he won't let that happen."

"We'll see." Slocum roughly shoved him to a seat on the ground. He noticed Blue Feather coming on the run.

"I think Hawkins is coming," she said. "Fast with two more men."

"Get ready!" Slocum shouted as the first light of day began to spread down the valley.

As he rushed for his horse and the Sharps rifle, he saw both Young and Milton nod in agreement. They'd heard the boy. Both gave him rueful looks and then drew their recovered pistols to get ready for the outlaws. Slocum left them; they had heard all they needed to know about the L and L Company. He slid the heavy gun out of the boot, took a handful of cartridges from the saddlebags, and went back to join Rip, the lawmen, and Blue Feather's forces lined up in the trees along the road.

The drum of hooves drew closer in the night. Slocum checked the .50-caliber's chamber. He inserted a shell and closed the breech. The oncoming riders were in a big hurry. By the sound of the hard-breathing horses Slocum judged that Hawkins and his gang had been riding hard a long ways. Then he could hear the squeak of the leather and the hoofbeats. Grateful for the moon, he knew that the riders would be in the light and his help in the shadows.

He fired a round in the air with his pistol, shoved it in his belt, and then stepped out in the open with the big gun leveled at the leader. Would they halt?

Black Dog looked both right and left with every intention in the world to escape, but there were no openings and so he reined up his horse. He slowly raised his arms. The others piled into him.

"Throw down your guns!" Slocum ordered.

The breed looked around, seeing the Shoshone women coming with bows drawn back, and the four armed white men; he spit contemptuously, then cursed them. With a wry scowl on his face, he dismounted.

"Slocum, what the hell is your game?" the breed asked.

"Justice," Slocum said, amused as he uncocked the Sharps and removed the shell. "Where's Hawkins and the whiskey train? I don't see some of your finer friends here." He gestured toward the other two.

"Get screwed, Slocum. You ain't holding me in no jail anyway."

"Where's Hawkins? You taking this jail time alone?" Slocum asked.

The breed just shrugged. Rip stepped in and handcuffed Black Dog with the lawmen's manacles.

"It won't be bad swinging without your old buddy Hawkins," Rip said in the outlaw's face.

The outlaw had no words, but Slocum read the anger on his dark face. Rip whirled Black Dog around without ceremony and shoved him toward the others.

"You ain't no federal law dog," the breed snarled.

"No, but I can cave your head in with my pistol butt if you keep mouthing," Rip said.

"The whiskey must be coming behind them," Blue Feather said.

"Must be," Slocum said. "I think the marshals have enough. They have these three, McFarland, Bailey, and the boy—whatever they do with him."

"They do not like the fact you had that boy who is bound?" she asked under her breath.

"No, his father is another chief in tribe. They fear his wrath!"

"I understand. What will you do?" she asked.

"We'll go find Hawkins and the whiskey. Then I won't be around when the lawmen have to decide if I can leave or not."

She nodded her understanding.

"Gentlemen," Slocum said, crossing to where the two marshals and Rip stood talking, "Hawkins and the whiskey peddlers that work for him are still out there. I say you take these prisoners back to Cheyenne. Rip and I'll get the others rounded up with the Shoshone women, and we'll bring them to you."

Slocum wondered how they would answer him about parting company. The time was at hand; either they let him go after the whiskey bunch or not.

"How about the matter of the warrant?" Rip asked Slocum.

"Marshal Young is clearing your name when he gets back, so you and Lucia can go home when this is over," Slocum said.

The lawman nodded, accepting Rip's thanks. "We'll certainly do that, Bell."

"This isn't our doing, but this whole matter is a lot deeper than our superiors thought," Milton said.

"And when the snow flies, who will feed all these Indians that didn't get anything to eat?" Slocum asked.

"We'll try to get the Shoshones' beef replaced."

"Thanks," Slocum said. The two might not get it done but he felt certain they'd try. "You can do whatever you want with Lamont Landers," Slocum said, knowing the boy was a tough situation for the pair. "But I'd watch him like an eagle."

Milton looked around. "We'll probably be forced to turn him loose before this is all over. Sorry, but I can't see any federal prosecutor or agency touching him, as powerful as his father is in the Senate."

"That would be, in my estimation, poor judgment, powerful or not. You have Black Dog, his four men, McFarland, and Bailey. We'll get the others and send them to you."

"Fine." Milton stretched out his hand. "John Smith, we'd never have done this without all your help."

"Rip and the Shoshone women, too," Slocum said, exchanging hand grasps with the marshals.

"Yes, but thanks for your part," Young said with a deep inhale. "Hope we never are on opposite sides."

"I'll try to avoid that," Slocum said.

Slocum and Rip left the two lawmen with their prisoners. Blue Feather's women hurriedly broke camp.

Hawkins and whoever was left over after the snake episode must have the whiskey train, Slocum decided.

"I sent a couple scouts to find them," Blue Feather said as they mounted to leave.

"Screw you, Slocum!" Black Dog shouted, loud enough to shake the leaves on the cottonwoods. "I'll get you one of these days!"

With a shake of his head, Slocum dismissed the man's threat for Blue Feather's benefit and rode on. "The scouts are a good idea," he said to her. "We'll have the rest of his gang shortly."

The Shoshone women had quickly loaded their horses and were mounted. Slocum and Blue Feather rode at the head of the column. Slocum looked around for Rip but decided he'd catch up in a short while.

Rip acted beside himself when he reached the two of them on horseback. He turned and twisted in the saddle a dozen times before Slocum asked what was wrong.

"I'm worried about Lucia."

"She's fine."

"Wish I was so damn sure. I don't think she's ever been pregnant before."

Slocum shook his head. "She's a big, strapping gal. She'll be okay."

"What if I have to help her have the baby?"

"You've pulled a hundred calves, ain't you?"

"It ain't the same!"

"Close to that," Slocum said, almost amused at the man's concern. "Just as soon as we arrest Hawkins and these whiskey boys, we'll ride out there and get her."

"I sure am worried about her."

Slocum agreed; it was obvious. Blue Feather looked ahead as they rode on. She also appeared close to being amused at the man's upset, but she said nothing.

Midday, one of her scouts rode in bearing news of the outlaws. The whiskey men were camped ahead and must be awaiting word from Hawkins what to do next. Hawkins was not there. Only six men were in camp according to the scout, who looked from Slocum to Blue Feather for what they wanted her to do next.

"Tell her thanks," Slocum said to Blue Feather. "I want to try and shoot them up at long range like they tried to do me," Slocum said, hoisting out the Sharp's rifle. "Tell her to join us."

Blue Feather did. Slocum explained to Rip how he and half a dozen women needed to circle around behind the camp and cut off any who ran. They were only to attack if Slocum's long-range plan failed. Rip agreed that was the answer despite the eight or so women warriors who were ready to charge in.

Rip and six of the squaws set out to encircle the camp and cut off the whiskey bunch's possible retreat.

They waited for an hour. Then, satisfied that Rip and his warriors were in place, Slocum and the others climbed the rise to view the whiskey runners.

About the camp were stacks of small kegs bearing firewater and packs. The mule train and their saddle horses were picketed on a line. The smoke of their camp was obvious, so Slocum decided they weren't worried about anyone finding them.

A half dozen men lounged around the camp. Slocum noted Quarter Martin and the Kid, who was sleeping with his hat over his face. All Hawkins's dogs were there.

"What will you shoot first?" Blue Feather asked.

"The whiskey," Slocum grinned and set out several shells

where they could easily be picked up and used. He nestled himself belly-down on the blanket she had spread for them to lie on while observing.

"What will that do?" she asked under her breath.

"Watch," Slocum said, closing the breech, setting the rear sight, and then taking aim down the barrel.

The big gun roared, and a cloud of smoke drifted north-ward. The pile of kegs nearest the horses exploded into a fiery inferno. This caused panic to strike the line of animals, and they tore loose in random fashion amid the smoke and fire and exploding whiskey kegs.

Slocum shot into the next pile of wooden kegs, which quickly joined the blaze as the men raced about firing pistols at unseen enemies. Calmly, Slocum reloaded, watching through the smoke and fire until the last stash was in his sights. He shot again.

"What now?" Blue Feather asked as the final stack of kegs exploded.

"Round them up," Slocum said and winked at her.

Grinning from ear to ear, she clapped him on his shoulder. "To capture the bad agent was fine, but this was even better. The whiskey will never reach my people."

Slocum agreed, rose, and took the reins to his horse from the woman who'd brought the animal up. He thanked her. Quarter Martin might still want to fight down there, but not as bad as before, and neither would the others, Slocum felt certain.

Would those two marshals turn Lamont Landers loose? Slocum almost wished he'd let the Shoshone women geld the worthless boy. Maybe he could still do something to be sure the boy was prosecuted; Slocum wasn't certain.

For the moment, his biggest concern was to capture the whiskey runners. He booted the horse off into the canyon. The women on horseback came with him.

The outlaws in the camp below looked undecided standing among the smoking ruins of their cargo. Then Slocum saw Rip and the others come off the far ridge, and the fight seemed to drain from the gang members.

Quarter Martin threw out his gun in disgust and raised his hands high. The others, one by one, followed suit, coming out from the fire and smoke with their hands above their heads.

Too easy. The whole thing went way too easy, Slocum said to himself with his pistol in his hand as his horse came, stiff-legged, off the last, steep grade. He worried something was not right. Where the hell was Hawkins? Not at the agency, not with Black Dog, not with his whiskey train. Where was he?

14

"One-who-runs and the others can take these men to the marshals," Blue Feather said as they finished mounting the last whiskey runner on his horse. Hands tied behind them, they made a sullen, downcast lot.

"You're kinda like the rattlesnakes," Slocum said loud enough for the Kid to hear. "But I believe you boys have been defanged. Right, Muldone?"

"You did that," the Kid shouted in disbelief. A black mask of anger swept his face. "I ever get out of this—"

Quarter Martin just nodded like he had known all the time. He spit dangerously close to Blue Feather. "She is the one with powers. Black Dog worried about her all the time. He says she sees the future. How long will we be in prison, squaw?" The big man with the grizzly beard tossed his head in her direction.

"Huh?" The Kid blinked his eyes and strained at the tight wraps on his wrists behind his back.

"Tell him forever," Slocum said and rode in closer to separate them from her. "Black Dog needed to worry; the U.S. marshals have him in custody," he said to the pair.

Muldone never answered; he stared ahead. But Slocum knew how deep the hate went down inside the man, for both him and Blue Feather. No matter, a federal prison sentence would do lots for his attitude.

"See you, boys," Rip shouted after them as the women led the prisoners away single file.

"Let's get this man back to his pregnant wife." Slocum laughed out loud at his friend as he winked at Blue Feather.

"Well," Rip said, "it ain't like we had a dozen kids."

"Maybe you will now," Slocum said.

"I may just work on that," Rip said, and they loped westward for the Shoshone camp.

Long after sundown, Rip, Blue Feather, and Slocum arrived at the main Shoshone camp. The tribe turned out to hear through Blue Feather's translation all about the capture and arrest of McFarland. Food was served, and they sat around in a large circle discussing what came next for their people. The Shoshones acted very pleased that the crooked agent was gone.

Slocum was seated on the ground eating buffalo and wild turnip stew when more riders came. He rose to his feet expecting One-who-runs and the others. Instead, Pap and his bunch came in to the cheers of many.

"Have any problems?" Slocum asked as the man joined him.

"That's what that Billings asked when I drove them mares up," Pap said, taking a dish of food a squaw brought for him.

"What did you tell him?"

"Same damn thing I'm telling you. I made it, didn't I?"

"You got the money?"

"I sure did, and if we kinda hurry, we can get back to the fort and celebrate the hundredth birthday of this country. I ain't so interested in those damn Yankee speeches, but I could stand some good whiskey and a little hell-raising,"

Pap lowered his voice to a whisper, "with some of my own kind."

"I've got a little business to take care of on the way," Slocum said.

"We can do that," Pap said, looking ready to eat as he eased himself down beside Slocum. "What have you got in mind?"

"There is a mule shooter I want to even the score with and a sheriff needs some lessons in manners."

Pap stopped spooning in his food and looked up. "Billy be damn, I'd like a patch of hide off him myself. Where the hell is Rip?"

"With Lucia somewhere around camp here. I guess they've been apart a whole couple of days," Slocum said.

Pap halfway frowned, as if considering something serious. "Can they safely go home?"

Slocum explained the arrests and the promise he had extracted from the marshals.

"So you been busy yourself?" Pap asked, looking around for someone. "Say, since we're in so good with these Shoshones, I wonder if I could trade for another woman."

"What about Morning Woman?"

"A man can have two Injun wives," Pap said, as if he couldn't believe Slocum was even questioning his purpose.

"Guess you picked one out going up there and back."

"Sort of. Her name's Gray Duck; she's around here somewhere."

"You better talk to the chief."

"I'll do that," Pap said as a girl brought him another bowl of food.

"By the way, we didn't get Hawkins." Slocum looked at the man for his reaction. "He outslicked us."

"Shit!" Pap spit to the side.

Slocum looked over the girl serving Pap as she exchanged some quick words with the older man. She straightened, and Slocum saw the youth in her face and figure. Gray Duck was young, pretty, and smitten with Pap. Wife number two, no doubt, Slocum mused to himself.

Later that evening, Slocum stood under the stars and held Blue Feather in his arms. He rocked back and forth considering how he much he hated to leave her and go on. Hawkins was still on the loose. There was the money he owed Ames for the horses. The two U.S. marshals, out of a sense of duty, would probably come and check on his whereabouts after they delivered the Indian ring to the Cheyenne jail.

"You will leave in the morning?" she asked.

"You know, like the eagle," he said, making a winged motion with his arms.

"Yes," she said, then took his hand to lead him farther out in the sparse grassland. They stopped, kissed, then walked on until they came to a small lodge under the stars.

"Tonight we share this place," she said and ducked her head to take him inside.

At dawn, still somewhat groggy from their night of fierce passion, Slocum sat cross-legged inside the entrance and studied the pink flannel lighting of the world. The colors became more brilliant, until the sun burned gold across the land. He could stay with her people, become a man in their tribe, and no one would— No, he could not risk these people's peace as they made the hard change from hunters to becoming farmers and eventually something very close to white men.

"You ready to ride?" Pap asked, leading Slocum's horse for him.

Slocum stepped outside. Blue Feather was still asleep,

just as well, he decided, as he put on his hat. He buckled on his gunbelt and then found the stirrup and mounted. Waiting for them in the distance, two women sat their horses with two packhorses on leads.

"You're going to have your own tribe one of these days," Slocum said to Pap.

"Maybe, but I ain't got good news."

"What's that?"

"Black Dog got away from those lawmen, and so did that boy. I figure Black Dog will want our hides."

"How did you learn all this?"

"One-who-runs came in with the news a while ago. Guess they let that senator's son loose. Somehow, the best I could get out of her, the Kid got hold of a gun or someone slipped a weapon to Black Dog. In the fight, that crooked agent McFarland was shot and killed. The breed somehow managed to get away."

"Landers's boy, too?"

"Both of them are gone, according to her. What are we going to do?"

"Find that mule killer and that lawman who needs a lesson. I gave them Black Dog once."

"Guess they just couldn't keep Black Dog, huh?"

"That's Milton and Young's problem, not my worry. Let's ride."

Early evening, Slocum and Pap rode into Laramie, on its main street, fogged with dust from the traffic. Slocum wondered if the deputy would remember him. They dismounted, hitched their horses, then pounded the trail dust off their clothing before they went inside the saloon. The Elkhorn Saloon's interior was smoke-filled, and the piano player was making lots of music. Several customers were dancing, with the bar girls for partners. Slocum and Pap took places at the bar. Slocum ordered them each a beer and set the money on the counter. There was no sign of the mule shooter.

"See you made it back," Rose said and slapped Slocum on the stomach with the back of her hand. She gave Pap a wink and pushed Slocum over so she could get in the space between them.

"Set me up on the bar," she told Slocum.

He obliged her, and she crossed her stockinged legs so that from her knees down they were exposed. Slocum noted that her tempting cleavage was still about to spill out of the top of the snowy white dress.

"Where's your boyfriend?" Slocum asked, ordering her a drink from the bartender.

"Robert?" she asked, rubbing her hands up and down Slocum's arm.

"The one I lost the bet on."

She thought for a moment. "He went to meet some guy."

"Elijah Hawkins?" Slocum asked.

"Yeah, he's the one he works for sometimes."

"You know where they're meeting?"

"Sheriff Suggs's place. Why you always so interested in Waverly and not me?"

"Never you mind," Slocum said, using his finger to push a one-dollar bill between her firm breasts. He wiggled his finger on the way out to test the firmness. "Can you keep telling us that a secret?"

"Of course I will." She looked down to follow his actions while he inserted a second dollar. He took his time. Slowly he poked downward until the money vanished in the sea of creamy flesh. "Come back, we'll do this again, cowboy!"

Slocum tipped his hat and winked at her as he and Pap left the saloon. She pushed her bust up with both hands for his benefit and gave it a shake, but Slocum had other things on his mind when the batwing doors shut behind him.

"They must be having a big powwow at the sheriff's," Pap said as they stood in the darkness on the porch.

"Hawkins must know about his losses and the arrest by now. I'd like to hear what they are planning."

"Probably how they're going to skin us and let the buzzards have our guts."

"Not if I can help it. Let's find the sheriff's place."

"You better let me do the finding out. I'm the stranger in town," Pap said. "You've been here before."

"There's a cafe open across the street. Bet you can learn in there."

"I won't be long," Pap said and spit a stream of tobacco off the porch.

Slocum put his shoulder to the wall and looked around; no sign of the night marshal. He lighted a quirlie as Pap moved across the street in a shuffling gait. He disappeared in the lighted doorway, and Slocum waited.

Soon Pap's tall frame reappeared, and he returned.

"Learn much?"

"Suggs's place is the first above the bridge on this side of the river."

"You don't have to go along," Slocum said.

"I'll be there," Pap said. "I owe that mule shooter Waverly a good hit over the head."

Both men unhitched their horses and rode for the river. Slocum wondered how he'd handle Hawkins and Suggs. Bound to be an easier way than call them out. He liked things better laid out than a shoot-out that would only get someone killed.

"You reckon that Rip and Lucia are home yet?" Slocum asked.

"Those two lovebirds, they'll be a while getting back there," Pap said.

"I hope those marshals got that straightened out for them."

Slocum and Pap hid their horses in the brush below the road, where the Shoshone women had hidden theirs earlier. In the starlight, they walked across the bottomland to approach the outbuildings from the back.

They saw a light in the barn alleyway, and Slocum wondered if the men they sought were in there. Carefully, he and Pap slipped up close and listened to the hard voices in the barn.

"I'm headed for Montana!" The unmistakable voice of Hawkins. "Black Dog's going with me."

"I've got to get home. Do you know if I hadn't been Senator Tyrone Landers's son they would have held me for trial?"

"Yeah, we know!" Hawkins said, unimpressed.

"Both of you better get the hell out of here before those special marshals come around looking for the lot of you." Slocum couldn't see him from his spot by the barn wall, but he suspected the deep voice must be Suggs.

"Not me!" Lamont insisted.

"You, too," Suggs said. "Sonny, you better realize they know how Black Dog got his gun. You're an accessory!"

"Yeah but they can't—" There was a loud slap and then some spitting. "Why the hell did you slap me for?"

"You're on the run like the rest of us are!" Hawkins said.

"I'll just go back to Washington and straighten this out."

"You want to bet?"

"My father has power and influence."

"I don't give a damn, you're staying with me, kid. Your

father wants to be a big power, he can get us all four pardons."

A cold chill ran up Slocum's spine. Where was Black Dog? Was he out scouting the perimeter of Suggs's land? Slocum's hand touched the smooth wood of his gun butt—

"I got the horses ready." The guttural sound of Black Dog's voice from inside the barn drew a silent *whew* of relief from Slocum.

"What are you going to do about Slocum?" the sheriff asked.

"Kill the sumbitch if I see him. Or let Waverly do it right this time."

"Count me out of this Montana business, Hawkins," Waverly said. "They ain't got nothing on me. I hate Montana."

"Lamont here and Black Dog and I'll go to Montana. That whore ain't going to support you," Hawkins said.

"I'll find work," Waverly said, sounding put out.

"How you going to handle Slocum when he comes back?"

"Shoot his ass off."

"Not his mule?" Hawkins laughed hard enough to cough.

"Slocum's probably got a gawdamn U.S. deputy's badge by now," the lawman said.

"I don't give a damn!"

Slocum smiled to himself. *Hawkins, you will give one.*

"What are we going to do?" Pap whispered, moving in close to Slocum with his rifle at his hip ready for action.

"Let them go. We can get them on the trail safer than a shoot-out here," Slocum said in the man's ear.

Pap nodded. "We better get back to our horses."

"No." Slocum shook his head. "I may not be able to implicate Suggs in any of this, but I need to teach him a lesson. I want him to understand Lucia isn't his fair game."

Pap nodded he understood. The three men were mounted up, Lamont whining the whole time about having to go along with them.

"The trip won't hurt you," Hawkins said with a growing impatience ringing in his tone of voice.

"What if those damn Injun women catch up with us?" Lamont asked.

"We'll rape them one at a time, then cut their throats," Hawkins said.

"They're tough," Lamont said as if he doubted they could possibly do such a thing.

"What do you think, Black Dog?" There was a long pause. Slocum strained to hear the breed's response. "Well, you afraid of those Shoshone whores?"

"One of them," the breed said.

"Which one is that?" Hawkins demanded.

"The one called Blue Feather."

"You stupid blanket-ass sumbitch. How could she be any more dangerous than any other female?"

"She is." Black Dog said. "She is."

Slocum stood in the shadows with his shoulder against the rough siding lumber and silently agreed with the man.

15

"That the bell off his milk cow?" Slocum asked.

"I don't know what the hell you'll do with it, but that's where I got it just like you asked."

Slocum turned from scanning the dark house. Hawkins, Black Dog, Landers, and Waverly had left an hour before. They weren't really Slocum's main concern at the moment. Satisfied there was no one in actual pursuit, the threesome would leisurely move north up the Bozeman Trail. They wouldn't be hard to catch; Slocum's main goal for the moment was to teach the sheriff a lesson in manners regarding how to approach and act toward married women. Lucia Bell for one.

"You need me?" Pap asked.

"Nope, but thanks."

"I still don't know what in the hell you're going to do with a damn cowbell and collar."

"Use it on him. Watch me," Slocum said and looked both ways as he left the barn with the bell and crossed the yard to the fenced garden. He stilled the clapper with his fingers as he slipped through the gate. The corn leaves rustled in the slight wind, as he found a place in the center of the half dozen rows. He released the clapper and hunkered down. One swing, one dull ring, then another, like a cow gathering ears of corn. Slocum duckwalked a little farther and swung the bell again.

"Aw hell! Damn you, cow, how did you get in the garden?" Suggs shouted from the open window. "Get the hell out of there. Shoo! Get!"

Slocum rang the bell softly, as if the cow were continuing to graze at her leisure on the rustling ears. He heard more profanity when the sheriff came out on the porch shouting for the cow to get out of the garden. Suggs made an easy target in the white nightshirt.

"Damn cow, who let that blasted gate down? Get the hell out of here! Where are you?"

Slocum gripped the thick strap on the bell with both hands. With all his might he swung the bell downward. The blow struck the sheriff on the shoulder and sent him to his knees. Suggs groaned and held his upper arm.

"Who are you?" he said before Slocum struck him in the side of the face with the bell, hard enough to spill the lawman on his side. The bell rang, over and over, as Slocum repeatedly struck the man on the shoulders and about the head.

"Damn, quit! What do you want?"

Nearly out of breath from his efforts, Slocum didn't speak. His arms ached from swinging the heavy instrument, but he wasn't through with Suggs, not yet.

"You've got a bad eye for other men's wives," Slocum said finally.

"Hell, is that you, Pat? Pat Carrol, I swear I only laid with her cause—"

Slocum gritted his teeth and struck him again, bouncing the noisy weapon off the sheriff's head, causing the man to shrink down and hold his hands over his head for protection. Suggs moaned and cried, "What do you want?"

"Who else did you force yourself on?" Slocum demanded.

"Molly Satter, but she's nearly a whore. Is that you, Pat? Damn, you got me bleeding so damn bad I can't see you."

"Lucia Bell, what about her?" Slocum demanded.

"I never— Who the hell are you? You ain't Pat."

"Let's say I'm Lucia Bell's brother."

"Hell, I never—"

Slocum struck him again. Suggs would learn to stop lying. "You and Hawkins had a warrant sworn out to get rid of him!"

"Damn, man, I never— Don't hit me. You going to kill me?"

"If I wanted to kill you, I'd cut your throat while you slept. But if I ever hear that you bothered or threatened my sister or her husband again, you better have your will made out. Am I clear?"

"Yes. Yes, I promise I'll never. What are you doing to me?" Suggs asked as Slocum threaded the collar and clanging bell around the sheriff's neck.

"I'm putting this strap and bell around your neck so you don't forget!" Slocum rammed his knee into the lawman's back. He forced the squirming Suggs facedown in the loose garden dirt and pulled the thick leather strap into the buckle. A hard jerk and Suggs gasped for air.

Slocum rose up, let some of the raw anger drain out, then headed for the gate. Suggs made some coughing sounds as he tried to claw the collar loose. Slocum never turned back. The lawman's wheezing and harsh breathing didn't bother him. Slocum felt the night's threat was enough warning for the man.

Pap brought up their horses. "Strange damn things, what a damn milk cow can do to a guy in the darkness."

Slocum saw no signs from the man in the garden. He'd live. Maybe he'd remember this night for a long time.

Slocum swung into the saddle. He damn sure hoped Suggs never forgot this night.

"What next?" Pap asked quietly as they short-loped out of the yard.

"Waverly."

"The old mule shooter, huh?"

Slocum nodded. He looked back in the starlight at the dark ranch buildings. Suggs better have learned something.

An hour later, they found Waverly drinking whiskey in the back of the Elkhorn. He looked at them warily as they stood at his table, then he reached to fill his glass.

"May we sit down?" Slocum asked.

"There's chairs there."

"You Waverly?" Slocum asked, then looked around the room, as if he dreaded something, before he looked at the man again.

"Yeah, what's it to you?"

"Are you really the best shot in these parts?"

"I'm good," Waverly said.

"Can you shoot a dinner plate sailed in the air?"

"Sure, why?"

"Dammit, Doc!" Slocum said like he was excited as could be at the discovery. Slocum squeezed Pap's forearm on the table in his excitement. Both men nodded like they were beside themselves with the notion of a shooting contest.

"But can you do it at night?" Pap asked.

"A white one, I can."

"I got two bucks," Slocum looked around again as if he dreaded anyone hearing them talking, "says you can't hit it in the dark out there tonight."

"That ain't no bet," Waverly said, shaking his head.

Slocum jumped to his feet, and the chair crashed to the floor. "You saying our money ain't no damn good!"

"Sit down, mister. Of course your money's good."

Pap motioned for Slocum to sit down, like he was real concerned they'd attract someone else.

"Who's got the plate then?" Slocum said, sliding the chair under the table.

"You can buy one for a dime over at the diner," Waverly said.

"Doc," Slocum said to Pap, "you go do that and we'll be out front waiting."

"Two bucks, huh?" Waverly asked.

"You miss, you owe me two bucks and the dime for the plate," Slocum reminded Waverly as they hurried to the front.

"I won't miss."

"You might."

"I won't miss."

Outside the saloon, Waverly stepped off the porch and drew a long rifle out of its boot.

"Oh," Slocum said, subdued, "you use a rifle to shoot with."

"Of course." Slocum's heart stopped for a minute as the man opened the bolt and checked the cartridge. Then Waverly replaced the bullet. Slocum gave a nod of gratitude. Pap came back carrying the white plate. They met in the center of the street.

Waverly looked back at the saloon with an expression of impatience. "We got to hurry. My gal gets off work in a while, and I'm taking her to my place."

"Shouldn't take a minute. Now, how do you want Doc to toss that plate?"

"Have him stand over there and throw it straight up so I can see it in the sky."

"I'll get over here by the horses so I don't make you nervous or nothing."

"I ain't nervous," Waverly said, disgusted. "Get ready to throw it, Doc."

"I sure didn't want to interfere with your shooting none," Slocum said, backing up to the hitched horses, to distance himself from Waverly.

"On the count of three," Pap said. "One-two-three!"

The white plate soared high in the early dawn light. Higher and higher, with a slight wobble, until it topped the false front of the dark store behind Pap. The rifle exploded and Waverly staggered back. He dropped the rifle. His eyeglasses were shattered. The gold frame hung behind his left ear; his face was a mask of blood from the explosion. Crying in pain, he dropped to his knees.

Pap came across the street and past Waverly. "Think twice, boy, before you shoot the next man's mule!"

"It's you, ain't it?" Waverly cried out. "She kept saying you was coming around asking about me!"

Slocum swallowed hard as he handed Pap the reins to his horse. Without emotion Slocum looked at the man for the last time as Waverly blindly stripped the empty gold frames from his face.

"Find better friends than Hawkins, too," Slocum said quietly as they rode past him.

"Damn you, Slocum! Damn you!" Then Waverly began to cry out loud.

"They got more damn military in the field than I've ever seen." Pap shook his head as they viewed another large contingent of cavalry and wagons heading north. "What the hell's going on?"

"The big offensive they've talked about against the Sioux and Cheyenne, I guess."

"Oh hell, that's been going to happen for five years. Let's find us a scout and palaver."

"We're still cutting sign of those three, ain't we?" Slocum asked as they rode.

"Damn right. That cracked front shoe on that one horse they got shines like a diamond in a goat's ass. They're headed for the Rose Bud."

"So's the military."

"Hell, you heard the man. Hawkins ain't letting no redskins scare him."

"Say, there's a civilian scout, let's catch him," Slocum said.

Pap waved for the two women to come on with the packhorses. The four riders short-loped their horses across the sagebrush mesa. The scout pulled up and used his hand to shield the sun from his eyes.

"That you, Whitcomb?"

"Me in person. What the hell's going on up here?"

"We heard Elijah Hawkins killed you in Wyoming."

"Not a chance. What's happening?"

"Hell, the damn Sioux ganged up on General Crook and sent him packing his bags up here yesterday."

"Crook?" Pap shook his head in disbelief. "He's the toughest one of them generals they got in the field."

"No worry, we've got them in a trap. Terry is coming in from the northwest and Custer from the east. Crook is getting refitted, and he's coming from the south. We're going to squeeze their guts out in a few days."

"Yeah, so they can write up that golden-haired squaw killer in them Eastern newspapers like they did about him in Kansas."

"I better get my ass to work. That lieutenant is a tough one to work for."

"Tell them boys old Pap Whitcomb is alive and kicking."

"I will, Pap." And the scout galloped off.

"What do you think?" Pap turned to ask John.

"I'm not sure." Slocum reflected on the man's word. They had a three-pronged attack to capture the Sioux on the last good hunting ground left east of the Rockies. The only one worth a damn, not picked over like the rest. Thousands of buffalo were left in the region. With the grass strong, they would feed lots of Indians through the winter. However correct the plan sounded militarily speaking, the fact that Crook had taken a hard blow might ricochet the hostiles in another direction.

Later that hot June day, in silence, the squaws, Pap, and Slocum rode in by the rows of bodies wrapped in sheets that the enlisted detail were assembling for removal. Slocum had seen death before; he never found it easy to stomach. No one spoke for several miles.

"They still ahead of us?" Slocum asked, feeling a small amount of distrust in continuing farther.

"I see that shoe going to Montana." Pap leaned over in the saddle to point out the track, then he righted himself.

"Where will we camp?"

"Sweet Water," Pap said. "If we ride, we can be there by dark."

Late afternoon, they met a small company of soldiers and scouts coming from the north. Slocum was anxious to know if they had seen two white men and a breed. He recognized the older lieutenant from Fort Laramie. Something was wrong, Slocum felt certain; the men had a blank look about them. They looked spooked, and even the officer in charge looked subdued.

"You going north?" the lieutenant asked.

"Yes, we're trailing three outlaws—two white men and a breed."

"You may not want to go due north," the officer said gravely.

"Why not?" Slocum rose in the stirrups and tried to see something like dust or telltale signs of war beyond the man.

The officer swallowed hard. "Colonel Custer and his entire command were massacred by hostiles just across the Little Big Horn River. We're returning to report the loss. It is nothing nice to see."

"How long ago?" Slocum asked.

"Two days. The bodies are mutilated and stripped. From the signs, there must have been thousands of Indians in this valley."

"Where did they go?"

"Tracks say in all directions. Excuse me, I must go now and report this to my commander."

Slocum nodded. The patrol trotted southward and left the four of them.

"What now?" Pap asked.

"Maybe my morbid curiosity, but I'd like to at least see the battlefield. We got enough daylight left?"

"I think so," Pap said and waved his women on.

Still later in the afternoon, they forded the swift Little Big Horn River; the water rushed around their horses' knees. Slocum warily twisted many times in the saddle to look around and check. The fire rings under the short trees were so numerous they shocked him by their sheer numbers. Lots of Sioux and their allies had been camped on the riverbank.

"There," Pap said and indicated the hill a half mile away where buzzards circled by the hundreds and magpies cried.

Slocum shook his head and tried to gather up some fortitude. "Pap, make the women stay here. The Sioux are gone. They'll be safe."

"Want them to make camp here?" Pap asked.

"No, the wolves will keep us on guard all night."

"Billy be damn, that's right. They'll be up here, too. Do you really want to go look at that?"

"I keep telling myself I'm man enough. But my stomach says no."

"Be history. Was it ten years ago that they killed Federman and his command not fifty miles south of here?"

Slocum nodded and spurred the big horse toward the cloud of buzzards. "Let's go see."

The last of the day's hot sun blazed on the death scene, covering the entire battlefield, from the lower slopes to the small peak of the grassy knoll as Slocum rode up from the river. The sour copper stench of death had already begun to gas the air. Slocum pulled his kerchief up to filter the bad smell.

Ten million buzzing flies fed on the less fortunate. Scattered among the stiff horse corpses were the naked white bodies of fallen men. Many were mutilated beyond recognition. Their eyes were missing, already pecked out by the birds of carrion. Many genitals were gone, eaten by the buzzards or sliced away by squaws who wished to deny the blue legs entrance into the life hereafter.

Shaken, Slocum had seen enough and left the hill at a trot. His nose burned from the stench. A large lump behind the base of his tongue threatened to force his jaws to hinge and to further force his stomach contents up.

"See Custer?" Pap asked, sitting his horse at the base of the hill.

"No, but he's up there," Slocum said and kicked his horse out for the women waiting by the river.

They camped several miles upstream. Neither man had spoken since they'd inspected the massacre. The sun sank beyond the Big Horn Mountains in the west. Slocum went down to sit on the riverbank, to be by himself and contemplate what he had seen. The Seventh Cavalry was gone. A lot more men had died in one battle during the Civil War, but this was a defeat of the U.S. finest by some ragamuffin hostiles. Slocum listened to the river. A dove hooted in the night. Then he heard the half-animal cries of something.

A man in rags—Slocum could barely make him out—came from the brush on the far bank, stopped unsteadily, and looked over his shoulder. He was making anguished animal sounds like someone in shock. Slocum had seen such mentally wrecked people before. They wandered off battlefields out of their minds, so severely shaken they sometimes even walked right into enemy fire. So gripped with fear they could take no more, they mentally broke down.

The man fell down and began to gulp water like he was dying of thirst.

"You hear something?" Pap asked softly, settling on his haunches beside Slocum.

"There's a survivor over there." Slocum indicated the man at the water's edge. "He's in shock. Just stumbled out of the bushes. He's drinking the river dry."

"We better get him," Pap said, shedding his boots.

Slocum agreed and pulled off his own.

The two were halfway to the man when he saw them. His bloodcurdling protest at the sight of them drew goose bumps on Slocum's neck.

"We're friends!" Pap said.

"It's Lamont!" Slocum said, hurrying through the water since Landers was nearly on his feet and ready to flee.

"Hold it!" Slocum said, catching the man's arm.

"No!" Landers screamed as loud as he could. "I'm a senator's son! He'll pay you!" He dropped to his knees in the cold water as Pap took his other arm and they dragged him to the south bank.

"Listen!" Slocum said, trying to break through the man's raging. "Where's the others, Hawkins and the breed?"

"Dead. The Indians got them! Oh Jesus, they killed them!"

"Are you certain?" Slocum asked, shaking him by the arm, for Landers acted so distant.

"Yes, they drove a spear through Hawkins!" Landers shouted at the top of his lungs. "It went in here," he indicated the sternum, "and came out his back!"

"What happened to the breed?"

"They tomahawked him in the head. Buried two axes in his head. Oh!" Landers went to crying, his whole body shaking with tremors.

"How did you get away?"

"They made me a prisoner. Oh!" Landers began to rage again with his own self-pity. "Those damn squaws—"

Slocum slapped him hard with the back of his hand and jerked him up with a tight grip on his arm. "How did you escape?"

"I stole a pony and rode away."

Slocum released his hold and let Landers slip to the ground, to ball up and sob some more.

"What now?" Pap asked as they walked out of earshot.

"You return him to Fort Laramie and demand a reward for bringing the dumb sonofabitch back. They'll pay it. I'm also giving you the money to pay Ames for his part of the horses."

"Where the hell are you going to go?" Pap asked.

Slocum rubbed the whisker bristles on his jaw. "Going to check on a Shoshone woman they call Blue Feather."

"That ain't a bad idea," Pap said.